"I'm adventurous," Raegan said.

"Would you like to have another adventure?" Alan asked.

"I do have to drive home," she said, beginning to relax as she gave him a wide, inviting smile.

"You don't have to drive home right away," he told her. "Actually, I wouldn't advise it."

"What would you advise?" she asked him.

"Well, what I would advise might get me slapped," he admitted.

She felt like her breath had just caught in her throat.

"Why don't you try saying it out loud and see?" she suggested. She had to focus on breathing. Even so, she never took her eyes off him.

Her pulse sped up.

"All right," Alan agreed quietly.

Putting his glass on the small table that had been brought in, he leaned in and placed his hands ever so gently on either side of her face. Cupping it softly, he brought his face down to hers.

He kissed her gently, softly, and as he did so, the sensation, the yearning within him, grew steadily more intense, more pronounced, until he finally drew her into his arms and gave in to the emotion that grew too large to contain.

Dear Reader,

Welcome back to Forever, Texas. This time, we meet Mike Robertson, his daughter-in-law and his three granddaughters: triplets Raegan, Riley and Roe. Mike and his neighbors are facing a long-running drought and the real possibility that the ranchers and farmers might very well lose their property.

Coming to the rescue is Alan White Eagle, who spent every summer until the age of eighteen in Forever at his cousins' ranch. During those years, he and the Robertson sisters, especially Raegan, locked horns over countless things. He's been gone for eight years now, earning an engineering degree. When his cousins tell him what they are going through, he comes out to see if he can help.

Despite their past animosity, Raegan volunteers to help out, working right alongside the man who had once been the bane of her existence. Come and observe what a difference eight years have made.

As always, I thank you for picking up one of my books to read. I hope you find it entertaining, and from the bottom of my heart, I wish you someone to love who loves you back.

Happy reading!

Marie

A Ranch to Come Home To

MARIE FERRARELLA

HARLEQUIN
SPECIAL
EDITION

HARLEQUIN®
SPECIAL EDITION™

Recycling programs
for this product may
not exist in your area.

ISBN-13: 978-1-335-40855-6

A Ranch to Come Home To

Harlequin Enterprises ULC
22 Adelaide St. West, 41st Floor
Toronto, Ontario M5H 4E3, Canada
www.Harlequin.com

Printed in U.S.A.

USA TODAY bestselling and RITA® Award—winning author **Marie Ferrarella** has written more than three hundred books for Harlequin, some under the name Marie Nicole. Her romances are beloved by fans worldwide. Visit her website, marieferrarella.com.

Books by Marie Ferrarella

Harlequin Special Edition

Forever, Texas

The Cowboy's Lesson in Love
The Lawman's Romance Lesson
Her Right Hand Cowboy
Secrets of Forever

Furever Yours

More Than a Temporary Family

Matchmaking Mamas

Coming Home for Christmas
Dr. Forget-Me-Not
Twice a Hero, Always Her Man
Meant to Be Mine
A Second Chance for the Single Dad
Christmastime Courtship
An Engagement for Two
Adding Up to Family
Bridesmaid for Hire
Coming to a Crossroads
The Late Bloomer's Road to Love

Visit the Author Profile page
at Harlequin.com for more titles.

Nik, Melany, Loggie Bear

And

The little one who is

On her way to join their family,

Sending you all

Oodles of love and kisses!

Mom

Prologue

Twenty-three years ago...

The knock on his front door caught Mike Robertson by surprise. It was after six. He hardly ever had guests come by his ranch even in the daytime, much less at this hour.

Since his wife, Amanda, had died several years ago, it felt as if all meaningful life had come a grinding halt. The sun had certainly gone out of his world...in more ways than one.

Ever since his only son, Ryan, had been a teenager, he and Ryan seemed to do nothing but lock horns at every opportunity. Without Amanda to act as a peacemaker, things had gone from bad to worse, until one day, he woke up to find that his son was gone.

After a fruitless search, Mike gave up looking for his son and forced himself to focus on running the ranch that had been in the family ever since his father had inherited it from *his* father. Ryan, he had convinced himself, would come back on his own in time.

The knock on the door came again.

For just a second, he thought it might be Ryan. But it hadn't happened so far, no reason to believe that it would now. Probably had to be one of the three ranch hands who worked for him, Mike decided. Given the hour, something had to be wrong. Hoping it was nothing serious, Mike got up from the kitchen table and made his way to the front door.

Sometimes, the ranch was more trouble than it was worth, he thought. Maybe he should just sell it and be done with it.

Yeah, and where would you go? Mike asked himself. Like the town's name implied, he had lived in Forever, Texas, all of his life. Not only that, but Amanda was also buried here.

He wasn't about to leave Amanda. Or the ranch. It was in his blood.

"Face it, old man," he murmured. "You're going to live and die here, just like your daddy did and his daddy before him."

The knocking grew more urgent just as he heard the crack of thunder. The brewing storm was all but on his doorstep.

Mike blew out a breath. Ever since his horse had thrown him over a year ago, he didn't get around nearly as fast as he used to and that really irritated him. It reminded him that he was getting old.

"I'm coming, I'm coming, keep your shirt on," he called out, preparing to give whichever one of his ranch hands was on the other side of his door a piece of his mind. At this point, he felt that the racket that was being created could have raised the dead.

Finally reaching the front door, Mike yanked it open. The words "This had better be good" were just out of Mike's mouth when he found himself looking not at one of his ranch hands, but at a total stranger. An extremely wet, *pregnant* total stranger who looked as if she should have given birth at least a week ago.

Normally, he would have guessed that the

weary-looking, dark-haired woman had the wrong house and would have said as much, but closer scrutiny showed him that the young woman wasn't just wet, she was perspiring. Not only that, but she also looked to be very unsteady on her feet.

Half a dozen reasons for her sudden, unexpected appearance ran through his head, the most logical of which was that she had run out of gas and needed help.

Mike couldn't ignore the young woman's flushed face. He had never been much for stilted politeness. He had more of a take-charge personality. It was one of the things that he and Ryan had clashed over more times than he could remember.

"Come in," he told her gruffly, gesturing into his home. When she swayed slightly, he was instantly concerned. Taking her arm, he led her inside, hoping she wouldn't pass out.

Not for the first—or last—time, he wished that Amanda was here.

"You want some water?" he asked once he had planted the pregnant woman in his armchair in the living room. He caught himself thinking that at her present girth, she easily filled all of it.

"Water would be very nice," the young woman told him, managing a weak smile.

Mike moved as quickly as he was able, going to the kitchen and filling a glass, then hurrying back with it.

He noticed that her hands were shaking as she took the glass from him and then raised it to her lips.

She all but drained it.

"Hey, steady now." Mike put his hand on the glass to slow her down. "I don't want you drowning." He was only half kidding.

Mike waited until she had swallowed and was able to talk. Looking at her with concern, the owner of the small cattle-and-horse ranch asked, "Is there anyone you want me to call for you? Someone who can come help you get home?"

The young woman was pretty despite the wet hair clinging to her cheeks. She shook her head.

"No," she whispered to him. "There isn't anyone."

Mike couldn't accept that as an answer. The dormant father in him rose to the surface. The pregnant woman in his armchair hadn't gotten that way by herself. There had to be a lover or boyfriend, or someone responsible for her condition, in the picture somewhere. Right now, Mike was willing to drag that errant man back here by the scruff of his neck to face his responsibility.

Studying the sad look on her face, Mike insisted, "There has to be someone, little girl. Tell me where he is."

The young woman's eyes rested on him and for some reason, a very strange feeling undulated through him.

A premonition.

"That's what I'm hoping for, Mr. Robertson," she finally said.

Mike looked at her, the uneasy feeling he was experiencing growing. "How do you know my name?" he asked.

The silence was almost deafening as he waited for the young woman to speak.

She took a deep breath before finally answering.

"Ryan told me." She saw Mike's eyes widen. "Just before he was deployed. I'm your daughter-in-law. Rita. Rita Robertson," she told him. "And these," she went on, cupping her hands lightly against her very large belly, "are your grandbabies."

Chapter One

Mike sat in his armchair, sipping his nightly single serving of tequila, just the way he had for years. Nostalgia had him reflecting on what an incredible difference the last twenty-three years had made in his life. Twenty-three years ago, he had been convinced that his life had reached a stagnation point. That there were no more surprises left.

Now, he thought with a smile, there were times that life moved so fast, he could barely keep up with everything.

And if Miss Joan hadn't dropped by on that

fateful day to check in on him and, more importantly, to ask to meet his newly acquired daughter-in-law, who knows how it might have all turned out?

He didn't want to think about it.

Miss Joan was the woman who had run the local diner since forever, as well as most of the lives of the people who lived in and around the town. There were those who claimed she had done both of those things since the beginning of time. It did seem like the woman had always been there and she had made it a point to be seamlessly involved in everyone's lives.

Miss Joan had certainly been indispensable to him when Amanda had died. She had made the funeral arrangements and took care of all the details when he couldn't even get himself to think straight.

And, he thought again, had the woman not been there that day, when she had come to meet Rita, who knew what might have happened?

In all probability, things wouldn't have turned out as well as they had.

As was her way, Miss Joan had marched into his house with her customary no-nonsense attitude, announcing that she was there to meet the young woman he had taken into his home.

For her part, Rita had been both happy as
well as nervous to meet this outspoken woman.

"Ryan told me all about you," Rita had informed the woman as she shook Miss Joan's
hand. She smiled at her, shifting a little. "He
spoke very highly of you."

If she was surprised at all, Miss Joan hid it
very well. "Well, I should hope so." Her sharp
hazel eyes seemed to take in everything there
was about the young woman. They came to rest
on Rita's belly. "When are you due?" she asked.
Coming from Miss Joan, the question didn't
sound intrusive.

"In a couple of weeks." Sitting near his
daughter-in-law, Mike couldn't help noticing
that the young woman's reply was accompa-
nied by a grimace.

Miss Joan frowned to herself, her eyes slowly
taking even closer measure of the young woman
sitting on Mike's worn couch.

"Well, you certainly look as if you're about to
burst right open," Miss Joan observed.

Rita smiled then. "That's because I'm having triplets," she explained simply to the older
woman.

"Still…" Miss Joan's voice drifted off as her

eyes rested again on Rita's more-than-ample belly.

And that was when it happened. A small, strangled cry escaped Rita's lips. Miss Joan moved forward, concern etched on her lined face.

As if it had happened last week, instead of twenty-three years ago, Mike remembered just how deeply worried he had suddenly become. His breath had caught in his throat as he had immediately looked to Miss Joan for help.

"Is she all right?" he had asked, his eyes darting back and forth between the pregnant young woman and the much older, wiser one.

Rather than look at him, he saw that Miss Joan had looked down at the floor just beneath his daughter-in-law's feet.

"As all right as a woman can be when her water just broke," Miss Joan answered.

Stunned, Mike suddenly looked around for the keys to his old truck. He drew a complete blank.

"I've got get her to the hospital right now," he cried.

Miss Joan was looking at Rita and obviously coming to a different conclusion.

"I think it's too late for that, Mike. The hospital is over fifty miles away." Taking the girl's hand in her own, Miss Joan encouraged Rita to grip her hand as hard as she could.

"What we *need* to do," Miss Joan went on, "is get her to a flat surface." She looked deeply into Rita's eyes. "It's going to be all right, honey," she promised the young woman. "This isn't the first baby I've brought into the world."

"Babies," Rita said, correcting the woman in an almost strangled voice.

"That just means that this is going to take us a little longer," Miss Joan told Rita matter-of-factly. "Judging by the look of pain on your face, this process isn't going to take nearly as long as you might think."

Mike knew that Miss Joan was just trying to calm down the mother-to-be.

Rita bit down on her lower lip, trying to stifle a scream of surprise, as another sharp wave of pain had obviously seized her before finally releasing her.

Mike looked at Miss Joan, as he had aligned himself on the girl's other side. Between the two of them, they wound up managing to get Rita to the sofa.

"I need blankets, towels and a pan of hot water," Miss Joan ordered, never looking away from the young woman, who was twisting from side to side, trying to find somewhere that the pain wasn't. "It's going to be fine, dear," Miss Joan promised in a gentler voice than Mike could ever remember hearing from the woman. "Just think yourself past this moment."

Rita had nodded obediently, unable to do anything else.

Thinking back now, it still managed to take his breath away at how quickly his late son's daughters had come into the world. One moment, he was hurrying into the kitchen to boil the water Miss Joan had told him to fetch and grabbing a blanket and fresh towels—and the next moment, he was hearing a bone-jolting shriek that turned out to be Rita's announcement that the first of her daughters had entered the world.

Hurrying back into the living room to bring in the pot of water, Mike was just in time to take the first baby from Miss Joan. He was wrapping the infant in the blanket he had brought with him, when the second infant was already beginning to follow in her sister's path, about to make her unscheduled appearance.

Miss Joan had barely had enough time to

throw off her coat before she had ushered the first of his granddaughters into the world.

And then the second.

Mike recalled not knowing what to do with the second baby. On occasion, he had helped birth calves on the ranch, but the newborn calves had always been able to get to their legs within a few minutes. He had never been faced with the dilemma of figuring out what to do with them once they had entered the world.

Again, Miss Joan was the one who came through with a solution. "Get that laundry basket you have," she ordered. "You can put one of the babies in there."

It occurred to him that Miss Joan was more aware of the way things were set up in his house than he was. But then, that was because Miss Joan had been friends with Amanda, and had spent time with his late wife while he off working on the ranch.

Holding the first baby in his arms and leaving Miss Joan holding the second one, Mike had gone in search of the laundry basket.

"Get back in here, Mike," Miss Joan called out. "I need my hands."

Hearing her, Mike had felt his stomach drop down to his knees, because at that exact second, he heard another, slightly lustier cry. He saw the half-full laundry basket out of the corner of his eye. He grabbed it just as he hurried back into the living room.

"Grandpa's sorry," he apologized to his first granddaughter. He put the infant into the basket on top of the laundry he hadn't had the time to put away.

He hadn't even told Miss Joan that he was able to take his second granddaughter. Miss Joan was already thrusting the infant into his arms.

"One more on the way in, Mike," she announced to him.

Unlike her sister, his second granddaughter was crying rather loudly. It was almost as if the infant was announcing the impending birth of *her* sister.

Unlike her two sisters, baby number three entered the world with hardly a whimper.

Rocking his second granddaughter in his arms to get the infant to cease crying, Mike looked over toward Miss Joan, a somewhat apprehensive expression on his face.

"There aren't any more of them left in there, are there?"

Miss Joan cleaned up the third infant quickly and placed that baby into Rita's arms.

"No, I think we're done here," she replied, wiping off her own hands. Miss Joan looked at the young woman on the faded sofa with compassion in her eyes, as well as her voice. "How do you feel, honey?" she asked soothingly.

Rita appeared barely able to draw enough air into her lungs to answer the question. For a second, her lips moved but nothing came out, causing Mike to become really concerned.

But then, one word finally did emerge.

"Exhausted," Rita whispered.

Miss Joan laughed, shaking her head. "I'm not surprised. I definitely would be if you weren't."

Still rocking back and forth, Mike was relieved. He had managed to quiet down his noisiest granddaughter. But he still felt somewhat shell-shocked.

"Three," he mumbled in dazed wonder. "Three granddaughters."

Miss Joan looked pointedly at his daughter-in-law. "Now you know that Ryan's father can count," she declared. And then she leaned in closer to the young woman who had just given birth to three babies in a remarkably short amount of time. "I have it on good authority that he knows how to read as well."

Had he not just shared an experience of a lifetime with the owner of the diner, Mike might have been tempted to put the woman in her place. But as it was, he was infinitely grateful to Miss Joan and knew that, no matter what, he always would be.

In the days that followed, his sad, not to mention lonely, world went from being numbingly empty into one that was so full, it felt as if it was veritably overflowing.

"I don't how to thank you," Mike had begun haltingly.

"Then don't," Miss Joan told him, waving her hand at him. "You'll just wind up embarrassing both of us. Better to keep your mind on these babies. They're going to require a lot of your attention, anyway.

"And don't look so spooked," she warned him. "Since there's no doctor in town, I'm not planning on leaving you on your own with these babies. I, or one of my girls," she told him, referring to the young women she employed as servers at her diner, "will be here every day until this young mama here feels like she can handle things on her own." Then Miss Joan affectionately brushed aside the damp hair that had fallen into Rita's face.

She smiled and looked into Rita's eyes, her own eyes crinkling a bit.

"That all right with you, honey?" he asked.

Rita smiled weakly, gazing down at the baby in her arms. "That's perfect with me," Rita answered.

"You're a good woman, Miss Joan," Mike said to the woman in what he willingly admitted was an uncharacteristically soft moment for him.

Miss Joan, now holding his last granddaughter in her arms, fixed him with what appeared to be a dark look.

"Don't let that get around or you'll ruin my reputation," she warned him. "Hear me?"

"Oh, I think that a lot of people in Forever already have their suspicions about that," he told her. He glanced down at the infant in his arms, and actually seemed to feel his heart skip a beat. "Look, look, I think this little baby is trying to smile," he said with a note of excitement.

"That's just gas," Miss Joan informed him dismissively. "And, if that little girl was actually going to smile, Michael, it would have been at me."

He knew better than to argue with the woman, especially since he felt so incredibly grateful to her. If Miss Joan hadn't come over to meet his daughter-in-law when she had, he had no idea what he would have done. The older woman's steady manner and expertise had managed to help usher in his three beautiful granddaughters while keeping his daughter-in-law as calm as possible.

He had felt at a complete loss as to how to make his thanks known to Miss Joan, other than saying the words to her over and over again.

It had been Rita who had come up with the solution. Each of the little girls bore Miss Joan's name as their middle name. So on their birth certificates, their names read Raegan Joan Robertson, Rosalyn Joan Robertson and Riley Joan Robertson. They had been born an incredible three minutes apart.

"I wish you were here, Amanda, so you could meet them…and they could meet you," Mike whispered quietly now.

It struck him as incredible that such a very important part of his life could have unfolded without his wonderful wife being aware of it or taking part in it.

The same went for his son, he couldn't help thinking. He had managed to have one final conversation with Ryan. That, he had learned, was thanks to Rita. She had been the one to convince his son that he needed to mend the broken fences between them—although he hadn't said a word about getting married, just that he had joined the army—and that he had a surprise to share with him.

Certainly had been a surprise, Mike thought now.

With all his heart, Mike wished that his son hadn't left home, hadn't enlisted in the army. Hadn't died. But there was no changing the past.

At least he could focus on the present and be thankful that his son had had the good sense to marry such a wonderful young woman like Rita.

Some things did have a way of working out.

Chapter Two

Hearing her approaching Jeep, Mike went to the front door, making sure that he opened it before Raegan could reach it. There was a reason for that. At one point or another, each one of the triplets had lectured him about his habit of not keeping the door locked, especially in the evening.

Quite honestly, Mike thought of himself as being old-school, going back to the days when no one in the entire town locked their doors and everyone was welcomed.

He missed those days, but his granddaughters kept insisting that it was better to be safe than sorry. He couldn't very well argue with that, he supposed. The girls and their mother were what he valued most in the world, and as long as they were safe, that was all that really mattered to him.

So if that meant going along with what they felt was so important, he'd do it. His concession to that school of thought was to lock the doors before he went to bed at night.

Although all three of the triplets still gathered around his table, usually several times a week, only Raegan and her mother, Rita, still lived with him. Riley and Rosalyn, who now went by Roe, lived in town these days, each one following her own career path.

He was proud of the way that Riley and Roe manifested their independence, but he had to admit that he missed the days when all three of his granddaughters were under the same roof. He had never realized just how much family really meant to him until, through the grace of Providence and Miss Joan, the girls and Rita had became such an entrenched part of his life.

Looking now only to prevent a lecture, Mike opened the front door just one moment before Raegan reached it.

"Hot enough for you?" Mike asked with a smile as he closed the door behind her.

Raegan rolled her eyes. She usually welcomed her grandfather's penchant for repetition, but that sort of thing generally involved stories about her father's childhood. She made no secret of the fact that she loved hearing those stories over and over again.

This just involved a trite saying that even hearing it twice was one time too often and she had heard that particular question far too many times.

The heat, she was willing to concede, was evaporating just about everyone's patience. Even hers.

She frowned as she took a deep breath. "It's even too hot for the devil, Grandpa," Raegan told him.

Mike stepped back into the kitchen and brought out a tall, frosty glass of lemonade. He held it out to her, his fingers making the glass appear as if it, too, was sweating.

"You should have come out of the heat sooner," Mike remarked, watching as Raegan all but finished the entire contents of her filled-to-the-brim glass. "Come over here," he urged his granddaughter, waving her over toward the sofa. "Sit. Take a load off."

Raegan slanted a look in her grandfather's direction. "I don't have 'a load,' Grandpa," she informed him, pretending to take offense. "In case it has escaped your notice, I am the lightest one of your three granddaughters." Although, she would be the first to admit, not by much.

Smiling, he humored Raegan. To his discerning eye, unless her sisters had gained weight in the last three days, since they had been here last, Riley and Roe were every bit as slender as Raegan was.

But his wife had taught him that women were extremely sensitive when it came to matters that involved their weight, so he always made sure that he held his tongue rather than get into those sorts of discussions.

Mike inclined his head. "My mistake," he freely acknowledged.

Since her grandfather had more than conceded the point, Raegan was more than willing to drop the subject. At that point, she turned toward the issue her grandfather had initially mentioned.

"You know, I don't think I ever remember it being this hot in Forever," she told him. "I feel like we're all trying to slog our way through an oppressive swamp. This afternoon, even breathing was an effort. And it hasn't rained since forever."

Mike laughed softly. "You certainly have that right." And then he said, "You should have come home earlier."

"And leave the other hands to fend for themselves while they tried to herd the cattle into some shade?" she asked. Raegan shook her head. "That wouldn't have been very fair of me, would it?"

Mike smiled to himself. Raegan had a wonderful work ethic—she always had. He was extremely proud of her. Actually, he silently amended, he was proud of all three of his granddaughters. There had never been a point that he wound up clashing with any one of the girls the way he had with Ryan.

Thinking back, Mike could remember that there were times when, if he maintained that the sky was blue, Ryan would immediately argue that it wasn't. They always seemed to rub one another the wrong way.

Heaven help him, even with them always butting heads, he still missed his son terribly and wished that things had turned out differently between them.

"According to the weather report," Mike told his granddaughter as he went into the kitchen, "this heat wave is supposed to go on for at least the next couple of weeks without any break in sight. Maybe even longer," he said with a deep sigh. "I'm not sure how much longer we'll be able to continue like this." He paused to look at Raegan. "I can't even remember the last time that it rained."

"Neither can anyone else, probably, except for maybe the weatherman," Rita said, adding her voice to the conversation as she made her way into the house.

Coming home from shopping at the general store, Rita was carrying two very large grocery bags, one in each arm, as she was attempting to make her way toward the kitchen.

Both Mike and Raegan were instantly on their feet, each taking one bag from the still very youthful-looking woman.

"You should have honked when you got to the house, Mom. I would have come out and gotten these for you," Raegan told her mother. "There was no need for you to have to try to lug these in on your own."

"I am still not all that feeble, Rae," Rita protested, looking from her daughter to her father-in-law. "I can pull my own weight. Right, Dad?" she asked, looking at the older man for backup.

Because her own parents had died when she was very young, Rita had gotten into the habit of affectionately calling her late husband's father "Dad." It had given her a sense of family and she suspected that it did the same thing for Mike Robertson.

"Absolutely," Mike agreed, referring to her comment about being able to pull her own weight.

Glancing toward Raegan, he gave her a warning look meant to keep his granddaughter from finding fault with what her mother had just said. He knew the girl's heart was in the right place, but Raegan wasn't at the point yet where her feelings of empathy outweighed her feelings of being protective.

Following her father-in-law and daughter into the kitchen, Rita waited for them to set down the bags they were carrying in for her and then she began unpacking them.

Her mind wasn't so much on the groceries that had been brought in as it was on what she had heard at the checkout counter.

"I heard something very interesting in town today," she told Mike and Raegan.

Mike knew that his daughter-in-law wasn't the type given to gossip, so he instinctively felt that this had to be something serious.

"And that would be?" he asked, looking at Rita.

His daughter-in-law turned from the bag she was unpacking. "Do you remember the name Alan White Eagle?"

The question had been directed toward Mike Robertson, but it was Raegan who reacted to the name first.

Alan White Eagle was a distant cousin of Garrett and Jackson White Eagle, two brothers who had taken over their late uncle's horse ranch and had turned it into a ranch that was devoted to helping troubled teens. They did it by teaching the teens to develop a sense of responsibility. Each of the teens would take care of the particular horse that had been assigned to them.

Mike had always felt that it was an amazing thing to watch the bond that developed between a teenager and a horse.

But right now, all that Raegan could remember was the endless teasing she and her sisters had endured thanks to Alan.

Especially her.

Every summer, Alan would come out to Forever to stay with his older cousins. Garrett and Jackson were typical boys, but they were polite, maybe because their uncle insisted on it.

However, Alan found a way around that whenever he could.

Raegan caught herself shivering without meaning to. She took a deep breath, reminding herself that it had been almost nine years since she had last seen him. Maybe he had changed. But if he hadn't, she certainly had. She wouldn't stand for any nonsense.

"Yes, I remember Alan. Why? Did he finally wind up landing in reform school?" she asked her mother, trying to sound casual.

"As a matter of fact, no, he didn't," Rita told her daughter, smoothing Raegan's hair away from her face. "Turns out he had quite a brain. He went to college, fast-tracked his education and now has two degrees, in the time that it takes a person to earn one. Garrett and Jackson always kept in touch with him and they told him about the drought we're having here. They also emphasized the way it's affecting everything in Forever." Pausing, Rita looked intently at the firstborn of her triplets.

"The young man is coming out to assess the situation, and once he does that, he's willing to meet with the local ranchers and discuss the options that might be available to them, as well as to the handful of farmers in the area so that they can keep their ranches and farms running," Rita concluded.

She looked from her father-in-law to her daughter to see what they each thought of the news.

"I plan to attend the town meeting when they have a date for it," Rita went on. "Either one of you want to join me?"

"You're going to attend a town meeting?" Raegan queried. "I don't remember you ever doing that before, Mom. I didn't think that was your 'thing.'"

Her mother was given to cooking and caring for her grandfather, as well as her. And her sisters, when they had still lived at the ranch. Her mother still fed Riley and Roe at least three times a week, whenever they did come over. Taking an interest in and attending town meetings was a completely new venture for her mother, Raegan thought.

"The town of Forever is my 'thing,'" Rita seriously informed her daughter. "And if something isn't done—and done soon—it's going to turn into a ghost town, because if the ranchers and the farmers can't maintain their ranches and farms, there isn't going to be anything left here."

This was the most passion that he had ever seen Rita display since she had appeared on his doorstep that rainy evening. Mike looked at his daughter-in-law with pride.

"I can see what Ryan saw in you, Rita. You do my heart proud," Mike told her. "Did you happen to overhear when this boy is coming to Forever?"

"If he has a degree in irrigation engineering, Dad, he's hardly a boy," Rita pointed out tactfully.

Mike chuckled under his breath. "When you get to be as old as I am," he said, addressing his remark to both of the women in his kitchen, "every man under the age of fifty looks like a boy to me."

"So I take it that you'll be coming to the meeting," Rita assumed.

Mike's eyes crinkled as he smiled. He had been doing a lot of that over the last twenty-three years.

"Count on it," he answered.

Raegan took in a breath. Although it was something that she hadn't particularly dwelled on over the last number of years, she could re-member every derogatory remark Alan had ever made to her. She definitely wasn't looking for-ward to seeing him again.

Ever.

But Forever was her home and she was will-ing to do whatever it took to help save it in any way she could. Even if that meant having to lis-ten to Alan White Eagle pontificate, which she was convinced that he would be doing.

"Count me in, too, Mom," she told her mother, doing her best to look cheerful about it. "Just tell me the date. And I'll pass the word along to Riley and Roe as well. I'm sure that they'd both be willing to attend the town meeting and do whatever 'Alan' thinks that the town should do to get us past this hump."

Mike looked at his granddaughter care-fully. There was something in her tone that had aroused his interest. "Is there something both-ering you, Raegan?"

"No," she answered a bit too quickly. And then she added, "I just wish that someone other than Alan White Eagle was going to be telling the town what their available options were in this particular case."

Mike exchanged looks with his daughter-in-law before he looked back at Raegan thought-fully.

"Well, we can certainly listen to what the young man has to say," he told Raegan. "The citizens of Forever are, for the most part, fair, intelligent people. If we don't like what we're hearing, or feel that Alan White Eagle really doesn't know what he's talking about, we don't have to do what he suggests. It's still a free coun-try, honey. But we do owe him the courtesy of listening to the boy...um, man," he told her, cor-recting himself with a wink.

Raegan laughed and shook her head. "Who are you and what have you done with my grandpa?" she asked.

Mike never missed a beat. "Haven't you heard? This is the new and improved version of Mike Robertson." He grinned at her.

Rita looked at her "oldest" daughter. "I'm sure that your father would agree," she told Raegan, then looked at her father-in-law as she put away the last of the groceries. "From what Ryan told me about you, he thought you were a tough 'old bird.' His words, not mine," Rita explained for Mike's benefit.

Mike smiled and nodded. He saw no reason to quibble with the words that his daughter-in-law had used. "We used to butt heads all the time. And after his mother died, it just got progressively worse and worse. Too bad I didn't try harder—too bad he didn't, either," Mike mused. "But we did have that one last conversation, thanks to you," he added. "I will always be grateful to you for that."

"If he hadn't wanted to talk to you, Dad, I really doubt that there was anything I could have said to make him call you." Placing the empty bag on the table, she made her way over to her late husband's father. "But I'm glad he did, too," she said. Turning toward Raegan, she asked, "Are your sisters going to be coming over tonight, or will it just be the three of us?"

"Riley said she would be here," Raegan answered. "As for Roe…" She lifted her shoulders in a shrug. "Who knows?"

"One way to settle that," Mike told his daughter-in-law and granddaughter. With that, he went over to the wall phone in the kitchen, the ancient fixture that the two women he lived with liked to tease him about.

He did his best to try to keep up with technology, but he saw no reason to fill his head with things that wouldn't really change his life all that much. He really had no use for a phone in his pocket. To him, it was an intrusion into his life, and there were enough things out there that already did that.

Picking up the receiver, he dialed Roe's number and waited for her to answer.

Chapter Three

It was midmorning and Alan White Eagle slowly drove through the little town he had visited every summer from the time he was a small boy until he had turned eighteen and had gone off to college.

He supposed he hadn't really expected Forever to change, even though he knew that was rather absurd on his part. Still, he was surprised to see that the town now boasted a new hotel and a brand new hospital to go along with the medical clinic that had just been a projection when he had left for college.

He hadn't really expected that either.

Everything always changed, Alan silently argued. Why should Forever be any different? His cousins, Garrett and Jackson, had told him ahead of time that things had changed in the little town.

Hell, even his cousins had changed, progressing from the carefree boys he had grown up with to the men who had taken over their uncle's ranch and turned it into a place that took in wayward, troubled young boys and turned those teens into worthwhile young men. His cousins had used horses, of all things, to teach those troubled teens a sense of responsibility and commitment.

Alan thought about it. He supposed that really wasn't so different from his becoming an irrigation engineer. Until he had made up his mind to go off to college, he hadn't had the faintest idea what an irrigation engineer even was. And now here he was, putting his degree to use to help save the little town where he had spent all those summers.

Who would have ever thought that things would take this sort of a turn?

But then, he wouldn't have envisioned that Forever would have ever had such a modern-looking hotel or an actual hospital housed within its borders.

Right now, Alan knew that none of those new changes would last—and that went for his cousins' very necessary horse ranch as well—if he couldn't put his education to good use and find a way to bring water to the extremely dry town and its surrounding area.

Alan's mouth curved ever so slightly as he thought about the situation that he found himself in. When he was growing up, he would have never envisioned himself as a rainmaker, the role that had captured his imagination when he had watched that old movie on TV.

He had watched, completely fascinated, as a flamboyant-looking Burt Lancaster had ridden into a little town whose citizens were willing to hand over their meager life savings to him if Burt would only live up to his promise to "make it rain."

Though he didn't remember the exact details, through the magic of Hollywood and faith, Burt had somehow managed to do just that.

Well, Alan didn't exactly need magic. He had his knowledge of irrigation engineering to fall back on. From what his cousins had told him, it had been extremely, not to mention unusually, dry for four months now in a place that ordinarily saw rain on a very regular basis.

At times in the past, Forever had seen even too much rain. Alan knew that from experience and the summers he had spent here.

He frowned to himself as he continued to slowly drive through Forever. He wasn't looking forward to addressing the town council about this dilemma the citizens found themselves in, but he did know there was a way out.

The problem was, the solution wasn't going to be cheap. But it could be done, he thought, and he looked forward to making it happen, as long as the people in Forever were receptive.

Belatedly, Alan realized that he had just driven past the diner.

On a whim, he backtracked, deciding to bring his vehicle right up to the diner.

But he found, to his surprise, that he had to park some distance away. Given the hour—it was just a little after six—he noticed that there were a rather large number of vehicles parked around and to the rear of the diner.

It seemed somewhat unusual.

Alan couldn't help wondering if today was something out of the ordinary. If perhaps the owner of the diner was celebrating some sort of special occasion, or if, because of the drought, people had gathered at the diner to offer one another some much-needed moral support.

Thinking back, Alan vaguely remembered hearing his cousins' uncle telling them that the town looked to Miss Joan for guidance when things were especially rough...or at least not going according to plan.

The drought certainly fell into that category.

The same whim that had Alan turning his car around after he had passed the diner now had him pulling up to the first space he found and getting out of the vehicle. After locking the car doors—living in Houston had taught him to be cautious—he walked toward the establishment, then made his way up the front steps to the diner's entrance.

Alan pushed open the door and was instantly enveloped by a sense of the familiar.

It was as if he had managed to step through a portal in time. He even thought he recognized some of the faces he saw at the various tables and at the front counter, although, Alan told himself, he was most likely just imagining things.

And then, without any warning, he heard her

voice. No matter what the situation was, there was absolutely no mistaking Miss Joan's craggy, raspy voice.

"Well, well, well," the woman said with a dry laugh, "as I live and breathe, Alan White Eagle. What made you come out of the woodwork, boy?"

Alan turned in Miss Joan's direction, clearly more surprised to see her than she was to see him—and this was, after all, her diner.

"Hello, Miss Joan," he greeted her.

Stunned, for a moment, Alan made no effort to come closer.

In typical Miss Joan fashion, she refused to put up with that.

"Well, come here, boy," she ordered. "I'm a little older than I was the last time I saw you and you still have legs that are younger, so you get to come to me instead of the other way around." In case he didn't understand, she beckoned Alan to come closer. "Well, come on, boy. Don't make me repeat myself."

Standing behind the counter, Miss Joan pointed to the space that was directly in front of her. There was an empty stool on the other side of the counter.

Miss Joan looked at him pointedly. "Come here."

As if suddenly coming to life, Alan inclined his head and murmured, "Yes, ma'am."

And then, crossing the floor, he made his way over to the spot where Miss Joan was pointing.

Satisfied, Miss Joan nodded her head. "That's better," she told the young man who came to stand before her, giving him what passed for her reserved approval. "So what are you doing back in Forever?"

Before Alan could answer her, the diner owner continued talking and asked him, "Are you here to save us?"

That question took him aback for a moment, until he remembered that even as a little boy, he had believed that Miss Joan had a way of knowing everything that was about to happen before anyone else did. He had thought of her as a witch when he had been a little boy. He still wasn't all that sure that she wasn't.

Alan slid onto the empty seat that was at the counter.

"I see you still have it," he told Miss Joan with a smile.

She cocked her head, hazel eyes holding him

prisoner. "I still have what?" Miss Joan asked him, curious.

"Your ability to know about things before they became public knowledge," Alan answered. He paused as the woman set down a cup of black coffee before him and then moved a container of cream right next to it. "Like now," he added with a smile, indicating the coffee and creamer.

"You're in a diner. Thinking you might enjoy having a cup of coffee isn't exactly a giant leap into the unknown," Miss Joan told him.

It was more complicated than that, he thought. "You put out creamer, but no sugar," Alan pointed out. "Usually, it's either both, or none."

Miss Joan lifted her shoulders, then let them drop in response to his conclusion. She made it seem as if her reply was a given.

"I remember things about my customers," she told him.

"Even if they haven't been to the diner in nine years?" Alan asked.

"Eight and three quarter years," Miss Joan corrected. "And, yes, even then," she told him. Then she pointed out, "You still haven't answered my question. Did you come back here to save us?"

Alan decided to play along for a moment.

"And what makes you think I can do that?" he asked the woman, curious as to just how much Miss Joan actually knew about him—or was she just giving the situation her best guess?

He was inclined to think it was the former, rather than the latter.

"Well, we're in the middle of a soul-sucking drought and I happen to know that you have a degree in irrigation engineering. It wouldn't exactly take a rocket scientist to put the two things together," Miss Joan informed him with a knowing look. "When are you planning on walking into the lion's den?"

Like everyone else, Alan had no idea how old Miss Joan actually was, but whatever the woman's age was, it was easy to see that she was still just as sharp ever. But right now, the question the woman had just asked managed to have him at a loss for words.

"Excuse me?"

"The lion's den," Miss Joan repeated. "The town council meeting. C'mon, boy, you're sharper than that. Keep up," the woman urged. "Tell you what, let me have Angel fix you up some of her famous pot roast. I've found that most men manage to think a lot better when their stomachs are full."

But Miss Joan had already said something that had caught Alan's attention.

"Angel?" he asked. During all the summers he had spent in Forever, he had managed to get to know all of its citizens to a lesser or greater degree. He didn't recall anyone in town named Angel.

"Angel Rodriguez," Miss Joan told him. "She came to Forever after you left for college. She's married to Gabe, one of the sheriff's deputies," Miss Joan continued to explain, then added, "Angel just happens to be one of the best cooks west of the Mississippi."

That was a pretty heady compliment, Alan couldn't help thinking.

Unless something had changed drastically, he remembered that Miss Joan didn't throw compliments around lightly—or for that matter, at all—most of the time. If the woman spared a few flattering words, appearing to send them in a person's direction perhaps without thinking, that was very high praise indeed.

"Well then, I guess I had better try this Angel Rodriguez's pot roast," Alan said to the owner of the diner.

Miss Joan nodded, already on her way toward the order counter at the rear of the diner. "Unless you've suddenly become feebleminded," she agreed, then eyed him. "Have you?"

"No, ma'am, I have not," Alan told her with an amused smile.

"Good to know," Miss Joan remarked, then added in a slightly lower voice, "I didn't think so." After ordering the dinner she had suggested to him, Miss Joan retraced her steps back to Alan. "Town meeting will be held this Tuesday. Will you be ready by then?"

He didn't ask her how she knew when the next meeting would be held. Garrett had told him that the meetings were held sporadically when someone in authority called for them. Alan had no doubt that Miss Joan fit that description to a tee. Instead, he just nodded in response to the question the woman had put to him. "I guess I'll have to be."

Miss Joan smiled her approval. "Good answer," she informed him, then decided that perhaps she was putting too much pressure on him. "But if you find that you do need more time…"

It wouldn't do to have Miss Joan thinking of him as starting out this project by being a step behind.

"I won't," Alan answered.

Miss Joan nodded her approval. "Another good answer."

Alan remembered the first time he had met Miss Joan. It had occurred to him that the woman easily struck fear into the hearts of a great many of the kids who lived in Forever. He also took note of the fact that the woman didn't care to see that sort of a reaction displayed.

That was when it came to him that Miss Joan respected those who had a strong sense of self. She respected people, children as well as adults, who couldn't be cowed or intimidated. Alan made up his mind then and there never to display any fear around the woman.

At the same time, that didn't mean he was given to displaying any false sense of bravado, either. But Alan did know that he would always have to behave as if he knew what he was doing.

Eventually, he had found that the woman didn't make him feel as if he was incompetent. On the contrary, he discovered that he felt as if he was in control of almost any situation. If Miss Joan was going to be attending the town council meeting, he felt that would only bolster his confidence.

He heard a small bell being rung and then spied a plate of pot roast, mashed potatoes and green beans being placed on the counter between the kitchen and the diner itself.

Miss Joan glanced over in that direction.

"Looks like your slice of heaven is here," the owner of the diner announced. The next moment, Miss Joan retraced her steps back to the order window.

After placing the plate in front of Alan, Miss Joan remained standing where she was. The expression on her face was nothing short of expectant. It was obvious that Miss Joan was convinced that the young man would be well pleased with this dinner she had suggested to him.

"If you find that you don't like this...well, I'll have serious doubts about your taste buds, but I will bring you something else," Miss Joan promised.

"I'm sure this is going to be every bit as good as you promised it would be," he told Miss Joan.

The woman remained standing exactly where she was, watching him carefully. But then she did smile at him.

"So am I," she responded. Waiting a beat, she watched the first forkful disappear between Alan's lips. And then, after five seconds went by, she finally asked, "Well? Is it good?"

"No," Alan answered, swiftly bringing a censuring look to Miss Joan's face, until he added, "it's fantastic."

Pleased, Miss Joan nodded in satisfaction, then finally went to attend to another customer.

Chapter Four

Alan was accustomed to addressing a handful of people or so. Usually those people were seated around a large conference table, and for the most part, the people he addressed had more or less the same sort of background that he had.

When he walked into the town council meeting, he scanned the immediate area. There looked to be a great many of Forever's citizens seated here—people who were invested in attempting to find a way to save the town.

People who were looking to him for guidance.

This was going to be tricky. He was going

to have to find a way to keep things relatively simple. At the same time, he couldn't sound as if he was talking down to them. Over the years, Alan had found that he had a great deal of respect for ranchers and farmers. They might not have the sort of degrees that he possessed, but they most definitely were educated in the ways of the world. He thought of that as having "life smarts," and when it came right down to it, he respected that far more than what could be gleaned from textbooks.

His cousins, Jackson and Garrett, and their wives, Deborah and Kimberly, were seated in the second row, right behind Forever's mayor and, surprisingly, Miss Joan and her husband, Harry.

Although she was a vital part of everything that went on in Forever, Miss Joan didn't usually attend the town council meetings unless the meeting was about a subject that tended to irritate her.

His cousins and their wives were there to simply provide their moral support. Garrett had sensed that Alan was somewhat nervous about the meeting, and Jackson had admitted to him earlier, just before he left for this meeting, they were all curious to see him in action.

Under the pretense of reviewing his notes

one last time, Alan slowly looked around again. When he did, he realized that he recognized a few more faces. Some of the other faces he wasn't too sure about. Most likely they were faces that belonged to people he guessed had moved to Forever after he had gone off to school.

Forever residents were still coming in and looking for seats. Alan waited for the crowd to finally settle down so that the mayor could introduce him.

Mayor Bradley? he asked himself, was that the man's name? The mayor had signed his name on the bottom of the letter that welcomed him to review the situation in Forever, but right now, for the life of him, Alan couldn't remember what that name had been.

That wasn't like him. Maybe he was more worried about this meeting than he'd initially realized. After all, this was the home crowd. The bottom line was that there was a great deal more riding on this than he had initially anticipated. He knew that a lot of people in Forever had sunk their whole lives into their ranches and farms, and their entire futures appeared to be tottering on the very brink of the outcome of what he said here, he thought.

Attempting to focus his attention on what

he was going to say, his eye was drawn to an extremely pretty-looking, dark-haired young woman sitting between a woman who looked to be an older version of her and a frowning, craggy-looking old man.

Was that Mike Reynolds? Alan continued staring at the man, doing his best to make the identification.

The name suddenly came to him, riding on a thunderbolt. Not Reynolds, but Robertson. Mike Robertson.

The name echoed in his brain like a revelation.

Did that mean that the extremely attractive young woman was one of the man's three granddaughters?

No, that couldn't be it, Alan decided. If he remembered correctly, the man's granddaughters were rather plain, maybe even a little funny-looking. This young woman with her long, flowing black hair could have been a contestant in an old-fashioned beauty contest.

Maybe even the winner, Alan thought, looking at her more closely.

Just then, their eyes met and Alan could have sworn that he felt something strange and electric in his chest. It was as if his heart had suddenly just skipped a beat. Given the rather reserved, stoic nature he had developed over the years, that seemed almost like an impossible assessment.

But he was definitely having trouble drawing his eyes away.

When he finally did, he realized that Miss Joan was observing all of this and taking it in, like a spectator at a show that was unfolding just for her.

"Yes," Miss Joan said as if reading his mind and answering his unspoken question.

"Yes?" Alan asked, sounding like someone who had wandered into the middle of a conversation he had no idea was going on.

Miss Joan shifted slightly in her seat, her keen hazel eyes taking in every nuance of what she had just witnessed.

"Yes," she repeated, "that is one of the Robertson triplets. The very same girls who you always teased so mercilessly every summer."

That couldn't be one of the triplets, he thought. Out loud, his protest took another form. "I have no recollections of teasing anyone mercilessly."

Miss Joan looked at him for what felt like, to Alan, a very long time.

"I'm not sure that Forever has any use for an

engineer suffering from amnesia," the woman told him matter-of-factly.

Alan exchanged looks with Miss Joan's husband, then decided that he needed to augment his original statement.

With a shrug, Alan told Miss Joan, "Let's just say I'd rather not recall teasing anyone mercilessly."

Miss Joan nodded her head. "Better," she told him, approving his new choice of words.

The next moment, Mayor Bradley rose to his feet and walked up to the podium. Sharp gray eyes swept over the crowd one by one until the attendees gradually quieted down.

Miss Joan leaned over toward Alan and whispered, "That's the way to get hold of the crowd." It was obvious that she viewed this as an object lesson.

Alan chuckled under his breath as he glanced at Miss Joan. "I guess I won't need my whip and chair."

"Not this time," Miss Joan confirmed. "But make no mistake about it," she went on. "You are going to have to win these people over."

He took in a deep breath. "I'll try to keep that in mind."

Miss Joan gave him a look that seemed to tell

him that he needed to do more than just try. The communication was silent, but Alan nodded, indicating that he already knew that.

By that time, the crowd had completely quieted down and the mayor began to introduce Alan with the legendary words: "I know that this young man needs no introduction." Bradley paused for a moment, letting the words sink in, then said, "We all watched him grow up, at least during the summers that he spent here."

The mayor paused again, then added, "Little did some of us realize then, as we saw him go galloping off with his cousins, that one day he would come galloping back into our lives to help us save the day." The mayor flashed a wide smile at Alan. "No pressure, son. Just a lot of crossed fingers," he told him. "That being said—" Bradley waved toward Alan "—I yield the floor to Alan White Eagle."

Alan rose to his feet, an easy smile on his lips as his dark brown eyes slowly looked over at the people who were waiting for him to come through with a solution to the dilemma that they found themselves faced with.

A smattering of polite applause greeted him as he came up to the podium. "I have very fond memories of Forever," he informed the residents who were sitting there. "This town has always been very close to my heart, even when my career took me elsewhere. So when my cousins, Jackson and Garrett, called to tell me about how badly the drought had affected the people here, I started looking into the problem.

"Most of you probably don't know that I have a degree in irrigation engineering—" he told the residents.

"Oh, we know," the mayor interjected. "Miss Joan made sure we knew." Bradley chuckled, glancing in the diner owner's direction.

Miss Joan responded by looking toward Alan, assuming the face of innocence.

Alan smiled at the woman, thinking back to when he had walked into her diner yesterday. He should have known.

"So what can you do for us?" Don Kelly, a third-generation rancher, called out.

He wasn't here to sell them a bill of goods. He felt it best to be honest with the residents from the get-go.

"There is no magic wand to wave," Alan told the residents. "The solution isn't a simple one." Several groans met his words. Alan had anticipated that and he pushed on. "But there *is* a solution."

"What, a powerful garden hose?" one of the farmers called out sarcastically.

That was when one of the triplets spoke up. "He came out here to assess the problem," she told the residents at the meeting in a loud voice. "Why don't you just let him speak?"

Surprised, Alan looked over toward the young woman. He had no idea which of the triplets she was, but whichever one it turned out to be, he felt grateful to her.

"Thank you," he said, nodding toward Mike Robertson's granddaughter, then with deliberately measured words, he began to explain the sort of solutions that the residents of the town were faced with.

Using what he congratulated himself as being basically simple details, Alan spent almost the next two hours outlining how they could irrigate the land, bringing water from the Rio Grande to eventually flow into a reservoir via pipelines in irrigation ditches. Those, eventually, could be used to bring water to the nearby farms and ranches.

Going over the details, he laid out plans to build an irrigation system.

Alan felt, he told his captivated audience, that the residents of Forever could never be too prepared for another, even possibly worse drought hitting these all-important farms and ranches.

"I know that it usually rains here regularly. But the specter of another drought is out of the question," Alan told his audience. "And the next drought could have even greater consequences."

"What about the price tag?" Jake Sullivan, one of the ranchers, asked.

"I won't lie," Alan told the man. "It won't be cheap. But this is your *land* we're talking about," he emphasized, looking at the residents in the front rows. "If everyone chips in, the bottom line won't be that overwhelming. And I know some other irrigation engineers who are willing to donate their time and bring some necessary materials to the construction sites to help turn all of this into a reality." Alan looked around at the faces of the residents closest to him, seeing how they took all of this in.

Pausing, he decided that he had talked long enough. The last thing he wanted to do was to overwhelm his audience or confuse them with his rhetoric.

Rather than ask the people in his audience if there were any questions, he told the members of the town council, "Why don't you take some time and think about what I've just suggested as the likeliest course of action? If it's all right with Mayor Bradley—" he glanced in the man's direction "—and the rest of you, we can meet back here at the same time in a couple of days."

Finished, Alan looked around the room to see if there were any objections to what he had just suggested.

There didn't appear to be any, so the mayor returned to the podium and declared, "Looks like this meeting is adjourned, folks. Like Alan just proposed, we'll all meet back here on Sunday." Bradley assumed his best smile as he told the residents, "Same time, same place."

Raising his brow, he surveyed the area to see if there were any objections.

There weren't any.

Alan began to move toward his cousins and their wives, but the mayor beckoned him over.

Not knowing what to expect, Alan made his way over and presented himself in front of Bradley.

"Good speech, Alan," the mayor told him. "I think you managed to create a lot of hope for these good people."

He was pleased, but Alan still shrugged off the compliment. "I'm just giving the people the facts, Mayor. I might not have spent my winters here," he conceded. "But I really do think of this place as home." Alan smiled as his cousins and their wives came over to surround him. "Some of my best memories were here."

The mayor nodded. "I can see that. See you at the next meeting," he said to Alan, then took his leave.

Out of the corner of his eye, Alan saw that Mike Robertson had risen from his chair. The rancher was escorting his daughter-in-law and the granddaughter who had come with him out into the aisle.

"You guys mind giving me a minute?" Alan asked his family. Without waiting for an answer, Alan quickly walked up behind Mike Robertson and the two women the man was ushering out of the meeting. "Excuse me, Mr. Robertson," Alan called out.

Mike turned and looked at Alan over his shoulder. Giving his daughter-in-law the keys to his truck, he told her, "Bring the truck around. We'll be right out."

The smile he flashed at the young man was wide and welcoming.

"Thank you for coming to bolster everyone's spirits," he told the young engineer. "Do you really think that plan of yours to access the Rio

Grande and bring water to the area is something that you will be able to accomplish, without it costing an arm and a leg?"

Alan nodded wholeheartedly. "It's doable," he answered. "How quickly depends on how many other engineers I can gather together as well as a few other factors."

Mike noticed that even though the young man was talking to him, the bulk of his attention seemed to be directed toward his granddaughter.

Raegan's two sisters had said they would be here as well, but at the last minute, something had come up to detain each of them. Riley and Roe had made Raegan promise she would fill them in on everything that was discussed at the town council meeting.

Since it was obvious that Raegan had captured Alan's attention, Mike made the necessary reintroduction. "I'm sure you remember my granddaughter," he began.

"Oh, I do," Alan answered with feeling. Glancing in Mike's direction, he asked, "Didn't you have three of them?"

"My grandfather decided that I was enough," Raegan quipped, overhearing Alan's question. "He gave the other two away."

Chapter Five

That was the moment when it all came together for him.

Alan could vaguely remember interacting with all three of the Robertson triplets. But there was only one of those triplets who won the title of being "sharp-tongued," hands down.

"You're Raegan," Alan declared.

Rather than act surprised that he could correctly identify her, or tell him that he was right, Raegan just looked at him innocently. "What makes you so sure?"

"Well, not getting into the fact that you've certainly blossomed in the last eight-plus years to the point that you hardly look like that young girl who used to taunt me all the time, I would still know it was you because I would recognize that sharp tongue of yours anywhere," Alan told her.

"*I* taunted *you*?" Raegan asked him incredulously. "Well, that's certainly not the way that I remember it." And then, with a careless shrug of her shoulders, she asserted, "I guess all that studying you did to get that degree of yours somehow managed to fog up the rest of your brain."

Her grandfather frowned slightly as he gave his granddaughter a reproving look.

"Raegan." There was a warning note in Mike Robertson's voice. "Remember, Alan is here to offer us his help. Don't wind up chasing him away."

For her part, Raegan's mind was flooded with all sorts of memories that didn't exactly bring a smile to her lips. Memories that nonetheless revolved around Alan.

She slanted a look toward him before she looked back at her grandfather. "I'd never want to do that," she told the man. "And I really hope that you're right about Alan being able to help the town, Grandpa."

Reading between the lines, Mike understood his outspoken granddaughter's hidden message. He remembered what these young people were like around each other when they were growing up.

He shifted his attention to look at Alan. "People change when they grow up, don't they, Alan?" Mike asked pointedly. "Otherwise, you wouldn't be here, volunteering your expertise to help us out, would you?"

Alan's mouth curved. "No, sir, I certainly wouldn't be," he confirmed.

"Well, like I said to Jonah earlier," Raegan said, referring to the farmer who had made the sarcastic remark about Alan before the meeting had officially gotten underway, "you deserve the benefit of the doubt. Even though," she added pointedly, "on a personal note, I have to admit that I hold everything you might say as being highly suspect."

Raegan paused to take in a deep breath before continuing. "But this isn't about you and me, it's about you and the good people of Forever, most of whom are desperately fighting to hang on and maintain their properties even while this whole area is being engulfed in the biggest drought they've ever encountered."

Most of the meeting hall had emptied out by now. Glancing over toward the door, Mike saw his daughter-in-law standing in the doorway, the keys to his truck in her hand. She had obviously brought it around to the entrance and was now waiting for him and Raegan to come out to join her.

Mike didn't wait to be nudged. "We have to be going now, Alan," Mike told the young engineer. "But why don't you come over for dinner tomorrow evening?" he suggested. "We can discuss your plans for Forever in a little more depth at that point. Are you up for that?"

He couldn't help but notice that Alan glanced in Raegan's direction just before the young man said, "Sounds good to me, sir."

Mike smiled at Alan. "With any luck, you're going to be able to implement solutions that could very well wind up saving Forever, so I think you can call me Mike."

Alan nodded good-naturedly. "What time would you like me to come over, sir…um, Mike?" the engineer asked, correcting himself.

Mike raised his eyebrows in a silent question, then asked, "Does six o'clock sound good to you?"

"That sounds absolutely great to me," Alan confirmed.

Mike nodded. "Then six o'clock it is." He turned toward the granddaughter standing next to him. "Let's go, Raegan. We don't want to keep your mom waiting," he said, prompting her.

"I'll be right there, Grandpa," she promised with a bright smile that was just a little too wide. "Just give me a minute."

With that, she turned toward Alan.

"We'll be waiting outside," Mike told his granddaughter as he moved toward the meeting hall's doorway.

Out of the corner of her eye, Raegan could see that Alan's family was drawing closer to him, so she began to speak, making her point as plainly and as quickly as possible.

"That man," she said, nodding toward her grandfather, "believes that you can do something for the ranchers and farmers in Forever. I just want you to know that you had better not be leading him on or you will regret ever having set foot back in Forever," she informed him through lips that were barely moving.

All the while, the smile she had pasted on her face never faded.

"Should I be afraid?" Alan asked, amused.

"I don't know," she said loftily. "Should you?" And then she reminded him, "My grandfather stood up for you. I won't stand for him being humiliated."

For a moment, Alan debated teasing her or saying something flippant. But then he thought better of the situation. It was important to make his position perfectly clear to Raegan. "I have no plans to humiliate your grandfather, Raegan," he told her seriously. "What I do plan to do is everything in my power to help him and the other people in Forever—" And then the smallest smile rose to his lips as he added, "Even you."

"See that you do," she told him just before she turned on her heel.

Raegan hurried out to join her grandfather and her mother, both of whom were waiting for her right at the meeting hall's entrance.

Watching her, the thought that Raegan was nothing short of magnificent floated through Alan's head.

She was also nothing short of annoying, but that particular thought took second place to his initial one.

With that, he turned toward his cousins and their wives.

"Sorry," he apologized, joining them. "I didn't mean to keep you waiting."

Jackson and Garrett exchanged amused looks. "Who are you?" Jackson asked. "And what have you done with our cousin?"

"Very funny," Alan responded. "It's getting late. Let's go back to your place," he suggested with enthusiasm.

Nodding in agreement, the White Eagle clan were the last people to leave the meeting hall.

Raegan found that she had to rush through her chores the following day in order to be able to attend dinner, which her grandfather had set for an hour earlier than usual.

Admittedly, everything within her wanted to slow down so she wouldn't have to be subjected to listening to Alan extrapolate on the subject of the drought and how he was planning on, most likely single-handedly, bringing changes to the area. She anticipated having to listen to him go on endlessly as he thumped his chest.

She knew that she just wasn't in the mood for that.

As usual, her mother was in charge of preparing the meal. Even so, Raegan needed the time to mentally prepare herself for what she felt was going to be an ordeal. After all, she was going to have to sit there and make polite conversation with someone who had managed to make her formative summers nothing short of miserable.

Raegan comforted herself with the thought that at least her sisters were going to be there. With any luck, they would carry the bulk of the conversation. Alan would probably still confuse them with one another.

She could remember times when they had been younger and they would decide to swap and take each other's places. That was when one triplet would pretend to be another triplet. Their teachers never caught on.

When they had done that in school a number of times, all the other students would think it was uproariously funny. However, their teachers were not exactly amused.

Neither had their mother been, Raegan recalled. The third time they had pulled that trick turned out to be the last time, she remembered.

Looking back now, she could see why the adults were annoyed. But at this moment, the idea of pretending not to be who she was carried a certain allure to it, as long as it kept her from having to interact with Alan.

Rita looked up from what she was doing when

she heard Raegan entering. "Raegan, could you please peel the potatoes for me?" her mother requested.

As a rule, Raegan knew that her mother prided herself on taking care of everything. She didn't usually ask for help or take it when it was offered.

Something was up, Raegan thought.

She noticed that Riley and Roe were out in the family room, talking to their grandfather. Since they had arrived earlier, why hadn't their mother asked one of them to pitch in?

But she decided just to go with the request rather than question her mother.

"Sure, Mom," Raegan answered. "How many potatoes did you have in mind?" She had a feeling that the usual number just wasn't going to do tonight.

"Twelve," Rita Robertson answered. "Come, sit by me," her mother urged, glancing at the place next to her.

Raegan anticipated what her mother was about to say to her. Her mother was probably afraid that she would get into it with Alan.

"Don't worry, Mom. You won't hear a peep out of me."

"I didn't mean for you to take a vow of silence, Rae. I just don't want you finding fault with Alan the minute he opens his mouth."

Raegan innocently batted her lashes at her mother. "Me, Mom? I'm not planning on saying anything."

Rita rolled her eyes and then laughed. "Oh, if only I could believe that," she told the oldest of her triplets. "You were the first one to talk out of the three of you—by a long shot if my memory serves, and it does."

Raegan continued peeling, but she raised her eyes for a moment and promised, "The rest of you can do all the talking. I just plan on listening." After slipping the seventh of the peeled potatoes into the pot of water, Raegan then crossed her heart.

Rita gave her daughter a look while she continued to prepare dinner. "I'm planning on holding you to that."

"I knew you would," Raegan told her mother with a good-natured laugh. "Besides, I've learned that the silent treatment can sometimes be far more effective than just simply stating an opinion."

The look Rita gave her firstborn said she didn't really believe that. However, all she could do was hope for the best.

"Why don't you peel an extra potato," she suggested to Raegan. "Just for luck?"

She had already peeled the twelve potatoes her mother had asked for. The extra one that her mother now requested had Raegan raising her eyebrow.

"That's an awful lot of potatoes," Raegan remarked.

"Better too much than too little," Rita assured her daughter.

Raegan felt as if she had just pulled double KP duty. "Anything else you want me to do?" she asked her mother.

Rita glanced at the peeled potatoes. "Cut them up and mash them," she told Raegan.

"Not that I mind spending all this time with you," she told her mother, "but why aren't Riley and Roe in here, helping with preparations as well?"

"Because if you're in here with me, I'm pretty sure that you will stay calm. If you're out there with your sisters—" she nodded toward the family room "—one of them might say something that could very well fan the flames of that temper of yours and just set you off."

Raegan frowned. "I'm not all that hot-tempered, Mom."

"I didn't say that you were exactly hot-tempered, Raegan. But I do recall that there was always something about Alan White Eagle that seemed to set you off," her mother remembered. "I would just rather that didn't happen today," Rita told her.

"Okay, now who's exaggerating?" Raegan asked, giving her mother a pointed look.

"I never exaggerate, Raegan. I merely observe."

"Maybe you were just observing the wrong triplet, did you ever think of that?" Raegan asked her, trying to look serious.

Rita laughed under her breath. "You forget, I'm your mother," she reminded her daughter. "I can tell you girls apart."

Raegan couldn't help smiling widely. "You know, I always thought that was an urban myth, Mom," she confessed. "And then Riley, Roe and I decided to play what we thought was the ultimate trick on you and we all switched places. Darn, but if you couldn't tell us apart.

"I honestly thought it was just pure luck on your part, but then you did it again. After the third time in three days, you turned me into a true believer."

Rita looked at her daughter, pleased. "That

just goes to show you, never doubt your mother, dear."

Having finished cutting the potatoes into quarters and subsequently putting the boiled quarters into a large bowl, she knew better than to think she was finally finished. "Anything else you'd like me to do, Mom?" Raegan asked.

"Well, since you've finished peeling and boiling them, why don't you mash them and mix the finished product with Parmesan cheese, butter and a smattering of salt?" her mother suggested.

Several minutes later, Rita paused to look over her daughter's shoulder at what Raegan had done. Rita nodded her approval.

"Looks very good, dear." And then she delivered her final suggestion. "Why don't you go upstairs and change into something a little… neater?"

Raegan looked down at the jeans and button-down shirt she had on. "Why? It's not exactly as if I've been rolling around in the dirt, Mom."

"Your sisters are both dressed for company, Rae," Rita pointed out tactfully.

Raegan frowned. "Since when is Alan considered company?"

"Since your grandfather invited him over for dinner," her mother answered. "Now scat.

Change your clothes before he gets here. Other wise, it'll look as if you decided to impress him at the last minute." She gave no indication that Raegan could opt out of changing her clothes, it was just a matter of when.

Raegan sighed, resigned to her fate.

"All right, Mom. For you—and just for you— I'll go change."

With that, Raegan went up the back stairs. The last thing she wanted was for her sisters to see her going upstairs to change her clothes. She had absolutely no doubt that they would grin slyly as they commented on the process.

Chapter Six

Alan pulled up in front of Mike Robertson's ranch house. He absently noted that even after all this time, the building appeared to be well maintained. None of the wood was splintered or peeling. As a matter of fact, it looked as if it had recently been freshly painted.

Still, he thought as he turned off his engine, this was not exactly the smartest thing he had ever done.

At the very last minute, Alan had debated bowing out by calling the rancher and asking Mike Robertson for a rain check. But neither lying nor behaving in a cowardly manner had ever been his way.

Besides, he had to admit that he was curious to see if Riley and Roe had turned out to be as extremely attractive-looking as Raegan had become.

Parking his vehicle, a dark green truck that he had treated himself to as a gift when he had graduated college with honors, Alan swung his long legs out. The truck was already used when he had gotten it, but it didn't matter. He'd fallen in love the minute he first laid eyes on it.

And now, despite the fact that it had a number of miles on it, the truck was still very dependable. It never gave him any trouble—unlike Laura, the woman he had been involved with in his last relationship. She had made it very known that she had no intentions of becoming an "engineering widow."

Telling her that his work came first didn't exactly qualify as his most shining moment, Alan thought. But in his defense, he really didn't like being told what to do and Laura Kincaid felt that since they were involved in a relationship, that gave her every right to dictate terms to him, especially when it came to spending their lives together.

The relationship had come to a crashing end shortly after that.

Thinking back, Alan had to admit that the relationships he had had over the last eight years hadn't exactly been long-lived.

But then, he thought the next moment, he wasn't really looking to settle down. What he was looking to do, Alan knew, was to make a difference, and this—what appeared to be happening in Forever—sounded as if it definitely could come under that heading.

Alan had already started up the stairs to the front door when he suddenly had to stop and retrace his steps, going back to his truck. He'd almost forgotten to take the bouquet of red and white roses that Jackson's wife, Deborah, had insisted that he bring along with him. She had even given him strict instructions.

"Remember to give those roses to Rita Robertson," Deborah had told him. "That will make you look good in Rita's father-in-law's eyes, as well as to Rita's daughters."

Alan had wanted to argue that bringing water to the parched area was supposed to accomplish that and that he really didn't care about looking good to Raegan and her sisters. But the words were no sooner on his tongue than he just swallowed them. Giving voice to that thought would have probably just given him away. He was better off just bringing the flowers.

So, avoiding Deborah's knowing look, he had taken the flowers and promised to remember to give them to Mrs. Robertson. It was a promise he realized that he had almost forgotten when he had left the bouquet on the passenger seat.

Holding on to the bouquet, Alan began to lock the truck when he stopped himself. He'd gotten into the habit of locking everything the moment he left it, because ever since he had gone off to college, he had lived in one large city after another. He had completely forgotten how laid-back Forever actually was.

He had to admit that it was rather nice to be able to be so trusting again, although it did take some getting used to, Alan thought.

Walking up to the stairs for a second time, this time he made it to the front door.

He rang the doorbell even though he suspected that the rather intricately carved door probably wasn't locked.

There weren't that many places like this left, Alan couldn't help thinking. Places where neighbors felt free to walk into one another's houses and leave their vehicles unlocked out front.

That was really a shame, he mused. Trust had truly become a lost art in most places.

The front door suddenly swung open.

Alan had expected to see Mike Robertson standing on the other side of the doorway. Instead, he found himself looking at a very attractive dark-haired young woman in a light blue peasant blouse and a soft matching skirt that fell well above her knees.

For a split second, his own knees felt just the slightest bit weak. And then, recovering, he looked down at the very attractive young woman's face.

"Hello, Raegan," Alan said, greeting her warmly.

"How do you know I'm Raegan?" she challenged. "After all, I could be Riley or Roe." Even as they had grown older, she was accustomed to the way the people in town were always commenting on how alike they looked.

"You could be," Alan willingly agreed, then said, "But you're not."

The sound of his voice got under her skin and that truly annoyed her. She gazed at the flowers he was holding but refused to ask whom they were for in case he intended to give them to one of her sisters. She didn't want to give him the opportunity to make her appear foolish.

Instead, she said, "You sound awfully sure of that."

His knowing smile irritated her even further. "I am."

"And why is that?" Raegan asked, an edge in her voice.

"Because only you have a dimple in your right cheek." Reaching out, he lightly traced the indentation with his forefinger. Raegan pulled her head away. "The other two don't."

Her eyes narrowed. He was trying to sell her a bill of goods. "I had the same dimple yesterday and you didn't seem to be able to recognize who I was then." Raegan pinned him with a look. "What's your explanation for that?"

"That's simple enough," he told her. "You were standing with your left side facing me, not your right." He smiled at her. "I have to admit that I forgot about that dimple until I just saw you now."

She wasn't buying it, and she was about to say as much when her grandfather chose that exact moment to walk up to the front door.

Just in time, Mike thought, because in his opinion, the most vocal of his granddaughters looked as if she was just about to say something that was less than flattering.

He dearly loved Raegan, but she could be extremely outspoken at times. Right now, the rancher felt as if Alan and the friends he had mentioned during yesterday's town-hall meeting were the best bet that the town had to survive this drought and its rather unnerving effects.

"I thought I heard the doorbell," Mike said by way of a greeting. Moving Raegan slightly aside, he shook Alan's hand and then nodded at the bouquet the young man was holding in his hand. "I take it that's not for me." Mike politely broached the subject without coming out to ask which of the triplets the bouquet was intended for.

Alan took his cue. "These are for Mrs. Robertson," he explained. "To thank her for all the trouble that she's going through to prepare dinner."

Mike seemed amused. "How do you know that I'm not the one who's making the dinner?"

Alan's mouth curved. "I guess I never considered that," he admitted. "Did you?"

"I didn't want to take a chance on chasing you away, boy. If this point eluded you at the meeting yesterday, Forever badly needs your help," Mike informed the engineer. "Come on in, Alan," he invited, then turned on his heel as he led the way into the house and toward the kitchen.

"Judging by the aroma, I'd say that dinner will be on the table very soon." Mike saw his other two granddaughters come in and then begin to greet Alan.

He also noticed that Raegan stepped back, quietly observing the exchange between Alan and her sisters.

"Make yourself comfortable," Mike urged the young man, gesturing toward the formally set dining-room table.

"Where would you like me to sit?" Alan asked, even as he smiled broadly at the other two triplets.

"You can sit between us," Riley told him, a welcoming smile on her lips.

Mike knew a problem in the making when he saw one. "Girls, why don't you go and help your mother bring the dinner in?" he suggested.

"I hope you like chicken Parmesan," Roe told him.

"I'm looking forward to anything that I didn't have a hand in cooking," Alan responded quite honestly.

Riley immediately picked up on what hadn't

been said. "You don't have anyone to cook for you?" she asked, surprised.

"I'm afraid I don't," Alan admitted.

That little piece of information was immediately greeted with wide smiles from two of the triplets.

For his part, Mike glanced in Raegan's direction. She looked as if she couldn't have cared less about the status of the engineer's life. That, in turn, had him thinking that a red flag had immediately gone up.

"Girls," he said, looking expectantly at the two granddaughters closest to him, the ones he had instructed to bring dinner back to the table.

No other words were necessary. "Yes, sir," Riley immediately responded. Meanwhile, Roe was already heading toward the kitchen.

"Raegan?" Mike asked, noticing that she hadn't taken a single step toward the kitchen.

"I made the mashed potatoes," she told her grandfather. "The way I see it, Roe and Riley can certainly do their part by carrying the dinner to the table."

Alan looked at Raegan in surprise. "You *made* the mashed potatoes?" he asked incredulously.

When she nodded in response, almost against

her will, she saw a smile blossom and spread out over his face.

"Funny, I just can't picture you being domestic and cooking," Alan said.

"Funny, I can't picture you using your brain for engineering purposes," Raegan quipped.

Alan appeared as if he was about to say something contradictory in response, but then he paused and merely inclined his head, as if in agreement.

"Touché."

Apparently, Mike thought as he smiled at the young man and his granddaughter, Alan had just called a cease-fire. He took the opportunity to call out to his daughter-in-law. "Rita, would you mind coming in, please?"

Rita Robertson came into the room in response to her father-in-law's call, wiping her hands on the apron she had draped over her dress. Going straight toward Alan, she beamed at the young man as her eyes swept over the flowers he was still holding.

"Hello, Alan. The girls told me you were here. Are those for me?" she asked, her eyes indicating the flowers he was holding.

"Yes, ma'am," Alan answered, holding the bouquet out to Rita. As he regarded the woman, it occurred to him that he was getting a glimpse into the future and what Raegan would look like when she reached this age.

Exceedingly attractive.

Accepting them, Rita paused to take in a deep breath. Her eyes instantly clouded over with tears.

Alan immediately thought the worst. "I'm sorry, Mrs. Robertson. Are you allergic to roses?" he asked, concerned.

"Oh, no," Rita said quickly, wanting to set him at ease. "I love the smell of roses," she confessed. A shy smile lifted the corners of her mouth. "They remind me of my husband," she told Alan. "He used to bring me roses when we were first seeing one another." Nostalgia entered her eyes. "He also brought me roses the day he proposed and the day that I told him I was pregnant. Roses have a lot of wonderful memories for me," she confessed. Rita took a second to gather herself. "Thank you very much," she said, brushing a kiss against Alan's cheek.

Watching this scene transpire, Raegan could have sworn that she saw Alan's cheeks redden for just a moment.

Wow, she silently marveled, *who would have*

*ever thought that the man was actually capable
of having feelings?*

Her mother turned toward her. "Raegan,
would you please put these flowers into a vase
for me?" Rita requested.

Raegan could feel Alan looking at her. He appeared to be pleased for some unknown reason
by her mother's request.

"Of course, Mother," Raegan replied. "I'd be
happy to." With that, she took the bouquet of
roses from her mother and went in search of the
aforementioned vase.

Rather than look at either one of her sisters,
or at Alan, she simply commented, "These are
lovely."

"I have to confess that the roses came from
the garden of my cousin's wife, Deborah," Alan
told the others.

"Well, she has a lovely green thumb," Rita
told him. "Be sure to tell her that we all said
thank you." She smiled as Raegan returned with
the roses, neatly tucked into a clear vase. "Especially me."

Alan nodded. "I will be sure to do that," he
promised.

"Well, shall we all sit down to dinner before
it gets cold?" Rita asked, looking around at her

family members and the guest her father-in-law had invited.

"I'm sure that everything will taste wonderful warm or cold," Alan assured his hostess.

"No doubt about that," Mike responded, giving his daughter-in-law a warm smile, before patting his stomach. "I was skinny before Rita turned up on my doorstep," he told Alan. "Skinny and very lonely, positive that I was going to go to my grave a lonely old man."

He smiled at the distant memory. "That just goes to show you, nothing is ever written in stone. For instance," he went on as they all sat down at his table, "a lot of the ranchers were convinced that not only was this the hottest summer on record for the last fifty years, but that there wasn't anything that anyone could do about the situation except wait for the inevitable to happen. And then suddenly, there you came, riding to our rescue."

"Let's not get carried away, Grandpa," Raegan said as she passed the bowl of mashed potatoes she had made over to her left, to Riley. "We don't know what he's going to do, we just have his word for it."

"That might be all well and true," Mike agreed, "but I have always taught all of you not to form any hard and fast opinions about something or discount it out of hand without the same sort of proof," he told Raegan as he looked at her pointedly.

"Sorry," Raegan apologized, directing her words to her grandfather, "my bad. I was just thinking back to years past," she admitted. And then she did look at Alan as she said, "Maybe you'll actually wind up surprising me."

Alan's eyes met hers as he accepted the platter of chicken Parmesan that was being handed from the other side. "I certainly hope so," he told her.

Raegan did her best to dismiss what Alan was saying to her and she definitely tried not to notice the warm shiver that insisted on making its way up and down her spine.

Chapter Seven

Because both of her sisters appeared to be fascinated with all the theories that Alan was advancing, they were asking him questions about the course of action that he felt needed to be undertaken. Questions about how to counteract the damage that the drought had caused and would continue to cause.

During all this, Raegan just kept silent. She allowed the conversation to be carried by Riley and Roe, as well as her grandfather and, of course, Alan.

During dinner, even her mother asked a question or two.

Finally Rita looked at the oldest of her trip lets. Leaning in toward her, she said in a lowered voice, "You've been very quiet, Rae. Is something wrong?"

"Other than the drought?" she asked, keeping her response deliberately vague. "No, nothing else is wrong. I'm afraid I just don't have much to add. I do want to hear more of what Alan here has to say about the methods he intends of use to get us out of this dilemma."

Raegan paused for a moment as she looked at Alan. "I can start a fundraiser going to collect money from the people in the town to help defray some of the costs for some of the things that you're proposing. That, plus I can get a lot of people involved in the physical labor part of this undertaking." She saw Alan raise an eyebrow quizzically, so rather than have him guess, she said, "You talked about building another new reservoir and you said that you're thinking about diverting water from the Rio Grande to help promote those irrigation ditches you mentioned yesterday."

Alan met her statement with a wide smile. She wasn't expecting that sort of a reaction from him. Had she gotten something wrong?

"What?" she asked.

"You *were* listening," Alan declared, pleased.

"You represented yourself as an expert," Raegan reminded the engineer coolly. "It wouldn't have been polite of me not to listen. That way, I could see if anything you said actually held water—you should only pardon the expression."

"And did it?" Alan asked. "Hold water," he prompted, curious to find out if she believed him, or just dismissed what he had said because she was being stubborn.

Raegan pressed her lips together. Much as she wanted to tell him that she thought he was just full of hot air, in good conscience, she couldn't. But she couldn't just bring herself to capitulate, either.

"I would like to believe that it does," she finally answered.

Alan's eyes met hers. A great deal of silent communication seemed to go on between them and Alan finally pronounced, "Good."

Rita decided to take that as her cue. She clapped her hands together, drawing everyone's attention toward her.

"Well, now that that's settled, how about some dessert?" she asked, looking directly at Alan. And then she smiled as she told him, "Peach cobbler."

Alan's face lit up. "You remembered," he said, surprised

Rita laughed, delighted with the young man's reaction. "Hard to forget watching a boy go through almost a whole peach cobbler like a buzz saw set on automatic."

"You made them on purpose," Alan said with an amused laugh. "And here I thought I was having this amazing stroke of luck whenever I walked into your kitchen."

Raegan exchanged glances with her sisters, then looked back at Alan. "I guess I missed the perfect opportunity to sell you a bridge back then," she commented.

Alan smiled at her. The smile seemed to say things to her, but at the moment, Raegan just couldn't put her finger on exactly what that was.

And then he compounded that feeling when he said, "There's always the present."

"If you two keep circling one another and talking in code like that, Roe and I are just going to have to eat both of your pieces of pie," Riley told Raegan and Alan. She punctuated her statement by flashing a pleased smile at their grandfather's guest.

"You two would never do that," Alan told Riley knowingly. "That's the kind of thing that

Raegan would threaten to do, not either one of you."

Roe exchanged looks with Riley. Her eyes were sparkling as she turned them in Raegan's direction.

"I guess he's got your number, Rae," Roe told the sister whom they had always considered to be the leader of their threesome.

Drawing herself up, Raegan rose from the table. "I'll go get the pie," she announced to the others, deliberately *not* making any eye contact with Alan.

Concerned, Rita watched in silence as Raegan made her way into the kitchen.

Entering the large, old-fashioned kitchen, Raegan realized that her mother had already taken the rather large, freshly baked pie out of the oven and left it standing on the counter next to the stove, covered. She guessed that her mother had covered the peach cobbler just before she had come out to greet Alan.

Raegan bit her lower lip. She supposed that Alan had to have spent more time at her house than she had realized…especially since her mother had obviously picked up on his dessert preference.

"Alan has turned out to be rather a nice young

man, don't you think?" Rita said to her oldest triplet as she stood in the doorway, peering into the kitchen.

Lost in thought for the moment, Raegan almost jumped, but she caught herself at the last minute. She looked over toward the kitchen doorway, shaking her head.

"You're getting to be a regular ninja, Mom. From the stories that Grandpa used to tell me about Dad, Dad would have been very proud of you," she said to her mother. "As for Alan turning out to be a nice young man—" Raegan shrugged her shoulders at the thought "—I think that the jury's still out on that one."

The slightest of frowns touched the corners of Rita's lips. "What is it between the two of you that sets you off this way?" she asked. "Your sisters don't seem to have anything against Alan."

"Maybe they're more easygoing than I am. Or more forgiving," Raegan added. "Or maybe they're just not as discerning as I am. Another possibility," Raegan mused, "is that Alan wasn't as sarcastic to them as he was to me every chance he got."

Raegan's last words had given her away, Rita thought. She looked at her daughter. "Don't you think you should set all that aside at this point?"

"When he gives me a reason to do that, then I will." She saw her mother's face. There was no such thing as a poker face when it came to her mother. All the woman's thoughts were always right there to see. "I'm not trying to make waves, Mom, but the fact of the matter is Alan used to enjoy torturing me and made fun of me every chance he got," she told her mother. "I found that rather unfair, seeing as how I looked exactly the way that Roe and Riley did."

"Maybe it wasn't about the way you looked, my love," her mother suggested. "Maybe it was a simple matter of your personalities clashing. Or maybe," Rita went on, picking up the peach cobbler to take in, "he was just being a typical boy."

Raegan's brow furrowed. "And what's that supposed to mean?"

Rita smiled at her daughter. "Since the beginning of time, boys have always teased the girls they liked best."

Raegan rolled her eyes. "Mom, that is so last century. Alan *never* liked me."

"I beg to differ, my love, but letting that go for now—" Rita set down the pie for a moment and then waved her hand at her daughter's last statement "—how do you feel about him?"

Raegan shrugged again, this time with a pronounced show of indifference. "I don't feel anything at all about him," she told her mother, then picked up the pie tin her mother had just set down. "Let's get back in there with this before they send out a search party for us."

Amused, Rita agreed, "Yes, dear."

Mike nearly walked into his daughter-in-law and granddaughter as he came into the kitchen. "What's going on in here?" he asked, looking from Rita to Raegan. "We are getting restless out there." He jerked a thumb in the dining room's direction. "I thought maybe something had happened to the peach cobbler and you were making a new one."

"The peach cobbler is safe and sound, Grandpa." To prove her point, Raegan raised the tin up to his eye level. "Mom and I were just talking about how little Alan has changed after all these years," Raegan said.

Mike glanced knowingly at his daughter-in-law. He had seen Raegan lock horns with Alan more than once since he had met the boy.

"Oh, really? Well, I know that he's really looking forward to that dessert, as are your sisters, so you'd better get a move on," he told Raegan.

Raegan nodded. "Yes, Grandpa," she replied docilely.

To her surprise, as she and her mother reentered the dining room, she saw Alan rising to his feet. That was exceedingly refined of him, she thought.

That meant that he had to be up to something, Raegan concluded.

Placing the pie tin directly in front of him, she nodded at it and told him, "Knock yourself out."

Alan smiled, taking his seat again. "This looks really delicious," he told Rita with enthusiasm, then added, "just exactly as I remember it."

"Thank you, dear," Rita replied. Picking up a knife as well as the spatula, Rita did the honors. She sliced the pie, cutting it into a number of pieces, and then distributed the first six slices onto dessert plates. "Raegan, if you'd pass out the plates," she instructed, "that would be a great help."

Raegan avoided making any eye contact with Alan as she passed out all the plates, then took the last one for herself. Only then did she raise her eyes to meet Alan's.

She was right. He had been looking at her the entire time.

Expecting to hear something on the flippant side coming from him, Raegan was surprised to hear Alan thank her.

Recovering after a beat, she replied, "You're welcome," just as she sat down again.

Not sitting on ceremony, Alan had already taken the first bite of his slice. The moment the fork disappeared behind his lips, he smiled broadly.

Watching him, Rita returned his smile, very pleased. "I take it that the peach cobbler meets with your approval."

The expression on Alan's face left no doubt that they were of like mind. "It's even better than I remember it," he told her with no small amount of enthusiasm.

Raegan saw a blush pass over her mother's face. "That's just your imagination, dear," Rita told him. "But thank you."

"No, he's right, Mom," Riley interjected. "This is even better than it used to be." She looked at Alan. "I guess we have you to thank for this. She hasn't made peach cobbler for a while now. I guess you're the special occasion she was waiting for."

"Then maybe I should come over more often," Alan told the others.

"Oh, hell, no."

Raegan looked almost more surprised than the others around the table when the words just slipped out.

"Raegan—" her mother chastised.

Alan's hearty laugh seemed to almost emphasize the moment. "That's okay, Mrs. Robertson. Raegan and I were always honest with each other." He looked at the girl he had once thought of as his personal archenemy. "Am I right, Raegan?"

For the first time since he had arrived and walked into their house, Raegan smiled at Alan. "Right. And since we're being honest with each other, I think you need to let everyone know the price tag that comes with this project you're proposing," she told Alan. "The faster we know, the faster we can start planning the fundraiser and start collecting the kind of money that will be needed to get this all going and off the ground."

"I've got a few friends coming in by the end of the week," he began.

"There you go, bragging again," Raegan interjected.

"Raegan!" her mother said sharply.

But her shocked disapproval was met by Alan's laughter. "That's all right, Mrs. Robertson. That's Raegan's way of pulling my leg," he told the older woman. Turning toward the oldest triplet, he asked, "Isn't it, Raegan?"

In acknowledgment, Raegan grinned, her eyes meeting Alan's.

"For once, you're right," she told him. "When did you say those 'friends' of yours were coming?" Raegan asked.

He thought of the last message he had gotten. "They'll be here by Friday."

She nodded. "Friday," she repeated. And then she looked at her grandfather. "Could you invite them to dinner?" she asked.

That didn't sound like Raegan at all, Mike thought. Just what was the girl up to? "You do realize that if his friends come over for dinner, he has to be here, too, right?" her grandfather asked.

"I realize that. This is a time for sacrifices and we all have to be willing to make them," she replied cheerfully.

Mike inclined his head and then said, "You heard my granddaughter—you and your friends are invited to our house for dinner." And then he glanced over toward Rita, since his daughter-in-law was the one who would be doing the cooking. "That all right with you, Rita?"

Rita smiled at her father-in-law's question. "That is perfect with me, Dad. I'll begin planning the menu now."

Alan nodded his head in response to what Rita was saying. "I've just got one request," he said, politely adding in his two cents.

To which everyone else seated at the table said in unison: "You want to have peach cobbler for dessert."

Alan grinned. "You all read my mind."

Chapter Eight

"Thank you all for dinner," Alan said as he looked around the table at the five other occupants sitting there. He rose to his feet, finally preparing to leave after spending a very leisurely two and a half hours sharing a meal with the family. "Everything was delicious, and I had a really great time."

Rita beamed at the young man. It wasn't often that they had guests. Usually "guests" these days referred to having Riley and Roe come over for a meal.

"You're very welcome, Alan. We loved having

you for dinner," Rita told him. Her eyes swept over her daughters for confirmation. "Didn't we, girls?"

"Not quite sure that 'loved' would have been the word I would have used, but it was nice listening to you go into detail about what you intend to do to help the town," Raegan said, rising along with the others.

Walking beside him, everyone saw Alan to the front door.

Pausing at the door, Alan nodded his head in response. "My pleasure. It isn't often I get to talk about what I do for a living with receptive people who aren't fellow engineers."

He was directing his words to everyone there, but in the end, his eyes came to rest on Raegan.

"Glad to be able to help broaden your horizon, Alan," she quipped.

About to leave, Alan shook everyone's hand and told them again that he was looking forward to seeing them again in a couple of days when his friends arrived.

Raegan's hand was the last one he shook.

He was about to walk out the door when Raegan said, "I'll walk you to your truck."

She'd managed to completely surprise him, as well as the rest of her family.

It took him a moment to come to, and then he said, "Sure."

Stepping back, Alan held the door open for her. She walked out and then they headed down the stairs over to his truck.

"You realize, of course," he said, "that if they find my body out here, your family will come to the conclusion that you were the one who killed me."

She turned at the truck to face him. "I have no intention of killing you…unless you're just raising up their hopes needlessly and don't have any intention of delivering on those promises. At which point, I *will* kill you," she told Alan with a completely straight face.

Pulling open the driver-side door, Alan looked at her for a long moment. And then he said, "I can't remember, were you always this violent, or was this just something that just naturally developed over the last nine years?"

"When it comes to protecting the people I truly care about," Raegan informed him, "I was *born* violent."

The smile that came to his lips in response to her words definitely worked its way deep under her skin. Raegan did her very best to block her reaction, but found to her disappointment that she wasn't nearly as successful as she would have liked to have been.

Moreover, Alan's liquid green eyes slid slowly over her face and she could have sworn that she actually *felt* his fingertips gliding over her cheeks.

Alan took what amounted to a single step closer to her, but somehow that one step completely erased the space between them as he smiled at her.

"You know," he told her, amusement shining in his eyes, "it's all beginning to come back to me now."

And just like that, Raegan felt as if he was using up her available supply of air. Although she was trying to breathe regularly, Raegan could swear that her pulse was beating progressively harder and harder.

What the heck was the matter with her? she silently asked of herself. She was behaving like some sort of dippy preteen, not like a woman who knew how to brand cattle, break in a horse and run her own ranch, if the need arose.

Her eyes narrowed into dark brown slits as she pinned him for his comment about things about her behavior coming back to him.

"Yeah, me, too," she told him curtly.

His smile deepened as it curved his lips. "I don't think that we're referring to the same memory."

"Probably not," she agreed, then told him, "I remember you being a colossal pain where the sun didn't shine."

Rather than her comment insulting him, she saw Alan nodding his head. "Maybe this should be the time for a fresh start."

"Okay," Raegan agreed. "But only if you live up to your word about helping the town," she told him.

He could have automatically just said yes, but he wanted her to be perfectly clear about this point. "You do realize that I can only do what I can do. There are other factors involved and although I can try my very best to make it all work out, I am not a magician." He saw her opening her mouth and sensed that something cryptic was about to come out. He waylaid her. "That being said, I want you to know that I am going to do my very best to bring water to Forever."

She sighed and rolled her eyes in an exaggerated fashion. "Oh, if only I could believe that."

At least for the moment, she almost sounded as if she was being sincere. "Well, that would be the first step," Alan conceded.

"What?" she asked. "Believing in miracles?"

"No, believing in the process," Alan told her, then added, "Believing in the science behind the process." He said to her in all seriousness, "Just so you know, I'm not planning on just snapping my fingers and bringing rain to the region."

"Oh, and here I was looking forward to seeing that," Raegan quipped. When she saw him grinning in response, she found herself forced to ask what he was grinning about. "What?" Raegan queried.

"You still have the same smart mouth that you've always had," he remarked.

For a second, in reaction to the way he was looking at her, her breath felt as if it was being stolen again. And then she responded, "If I have a 'smart mouth,' it's only in self-defense against you."

"You don't need to exercise any self-defense," Alan told her.

"That is a matter of opinion," she informed him. And then she deliberately changed the subject. "These friends of yours that you're calling in to help you with what you're proposing, are they any good? Or is pretending to work on irrigation ditches something that they do in between their actual day jobs?"

"Oh, yes, they are extremely good," he told her without a hint of a smile.

"Then why are they coming here?" she asked. "Why aren't those friends of yours working some big job in a more lucrative part of the country?" It just didn't seem to make any sense to her.

"Not everyone is in it for the money, Rae," he told her.

She didn't appreciate him using her nickname and she contradicted Alan. "*Everyone* is in it for the money."

"You know, I don't remember you being this jaded before," he remarked.

Raegan waved her hand dismissively at him. "Then you're not remembering things correctly because I have *always* been this jaded," she told him. And then she grew more serious. "Really, what is the asking price for your friends' help?"

She really was having a great deal of trouble accepting that these so-called friends of his were doing this out of the goodness of their hearts. Especially out of Alan's heart. She was approaching this pragmatically. If she knew what to expect, then she would know just how much money she needed to raise.

Alan had opened the door to his truck and had sat down behind the wheel. He looked at her now and knew that this needed more than just a flippant answer on his part.

"Why don't you come up and sit down in the truck with me?" he proposed, and then added, "Unless you're afraid to."

Her eyes narrowed. "Of you? No way," she informed him.

He knew she'd say that. He nodded. "Good to know. Then come on up and sit down in the truck." He nodded toward the passenger seat next to him. "I promise not to bite," he added.

Her eyes met his. "You wouldn't dare," she told him.

He laughed. "Ten years ago, I might have been tempted."

His eyes smiled at her. There had always been something about Raegan Robertson that had managed to get under his skin in a big way. He found himself sorely tempted to find out if her lips tasted as sweet as he imagined that they did.

But this wasn't the time for that, he told himself, as she walked around the truck, opened the passenger door and got in. He had been invited out here to tackle something very serious, and tackle it, he intended to. Tackle it and find at least some sort of an acceptable solution for these people, whose survival spelled "home" to him.

Forever meant a great deal to him. As he had said to Raegan's grandfather, the town held a great many good memories for him. His parents were always busy with their careers. During the school year, he was always being bundled off to one private school or another. There had been a number of schools in his life.

Spending summers in Forever had been the only taste of normalcy that he had experienced.

Leaning over, Alan opened the glove compartment in order to extract the old-fashioned notebook he had been writing in. He accidentally brushed the back of his hand against her and he noticed that Raegan was trying to press herself back against the passenger seat.

"Sorry," Alan apologized. "I just wanted to show you this," he explained, nodding at the notebook.

"A notebook?" Raegan asked, looking at him in surprise. "I would have expected you to be using the latest technology available, not something from the beginning of the last century."

He had come to look at things differently in the last few years, after seeing some of his intricate work suddenly disappear thanks to power failures.

"Technology can have all sorts of glitches assault it. I like pencil and paper." He looked at her, a self-mocking expression on his face. "Now you know my dirty little secret."

Like that was the worst thing he was guilty of, Raegan thought. "Oh, I'm sure there are others."

Rather than answer her, he allowed a smile to play on his lips for a moment, then began to explain the figures in his notebook.

"Once Jackson and Garrett called to tell me about the drought here, I started making projections of what things would wind up costing and what sort of corners could be cut to get the same sort of results without threatening to bankrupt the entire town."

Raegan flipped through the pages, looking at the various figures and projections that Alan had written down. Her eyes came to rest on the last figure on the current page, widening as she looked at the numbers.

"Is this the bottom line?" she asked in disbelief.

"No, it's the 'middle' line," Alan told her. "That number leaves room for any contingencies and things that could come up—the way that things always seem to," he explained. "Do you think the townspeople could handle this sum?" It was a genuine question on his part.

She looked at the notebook page again and blew out a breath. That was a pretty big sum for a lot of people. But, she supposed, it was all in the way people looked at it.

Raegan shook her head. "They can handle it a lot better than they can handle the lack of water causing them to lose their ranches and their farms, because the drought winds up having everything here burn to a crisp," she told him. Raegan closed the notebook and looked at Alan. "How many of your engineer friends are going to be coming?" she asked.

"Right now, not counting me," he told her, "there are three other engineers I've invited to work with me on this."

"Are they going to be staying at the hotel?" she asked.

He nodded, and then a thought suddenly hit him. "When did the town get a hotel?" he asked. There hadn't been a hotel in town when he had spent his last summer here. Just like there hadn't been a hospital.

Forever had certainly been growing, he couldn't help thinking.

"About seven years ago," she told him. "I take it you've been staying at the ranch with your cousins and their wives."

"For now," he admitted. "But I'll be moving into the hotel when my friends get here."

"Why move?" she asked. She would have thought he would welcome this time with his cousins.

"It'll be easier to interact with the other engineers if we're all in the same place. I can't very well expect Jackson and Garrett to take all my friends in as well, especially not while they have all those kids staying at the ranch with them," he said, referring to the runaways and troubled teens that were being housed at the ranch.

Raegan was looking at him thoughtfully as he spoke. "Let me talk to the hotel owners."

He didn't understand where she was going with this. "Why?"

"They might be willing to let you and your friends stay at the hotel for free, or at least at a reduced rate, in exchange for the work you all intend to do. As for eating," she continued, thinking along the same lines, "I'm sure that Miss Joan will let you pay reduced rates for your meals, and even occasionally foot the bill for those meals so that could help 'pay' you for your services.

"As for the cost of the materials for the reservoir, as well as for the cost of constructing the reservoir and the irrigation ditches to direct the water from the Rio Grande, that's where the fundraiser is going to come in," Raegan informed him.

"Then you were actually serious about that fundraiser?" he said.

Why would he think she wasn't? "Of course, I was serious. The people in town might not be as sophisticated as the people you're used to dealing with, but they're not expecting a fairy godmother to come and construct the reservoir, or to build those irrigation ditches to bring water to the ranches and farms."

Humor lit up his face. "You mean I wouldn't pass for a fairy godmother?"

She shook her head. "Nope. For one thing, your voice is much too deep."

Alan grinned. "You know, I think that's the nicest thing you've said to me since I came into town."

She couldn't help laughing. "Talk about setting the bar at a new low," she commented.

"All depends on your point of view," he told her. "There was a time when I would have practiced ducking, expecting you to stone me."

Raegan waved a hand at his so-called observation. "Things were never that bad between us. You just liked tormenting me," she reminded him.

"That was just in self-defense. You had a pretty sharp tongue."

"Like I said, all that studying you did just wound up clouding your brain. But let's not argue about that now. For the time being, we're on the same side and I would like to keep it that way. Deal?" Raegan asked, putting her hand out to Alan's.

He slipped his fingers around her hand. "Deal," he told her.

Acutely aware of the wave of electricity shooting between his hand and hers, Raegan struggled not to pull her hand away or give any indication of what she was experiencing…but it definitely wasn't easy.

Chapter Nine

"So? How did things go?" Raegan's grandfather asked.

When he heard Alan's truck pull away and didn't hear his granddaughter come back inside the house, he had decided to walk outside and see if she had left with the young man.

She hadn't.

"Were you waiting out here for me?" Raegan asked.

"No, I just came out now to check if you were still here," he answered, then pointed out, "You were gone for a while."

"I know," Raegan admitted. "Alan offered to show me some of the figures for what the irrigation ditches and building the reservoir were going to come to." She turned toward her grandfather and looked a little wistful. "It might just be a lot easier to get someone to set up an elaborate sprinkling system," she said sarcastically.

"You know, if that actually worked, I'd be all for it," her grandfather admitted.

Raegan laughed. "You and me both, Grandpa." And then she grew serious. "How do you feel about this?" she asked.

"'This?'" Mike repeated, looking at her for a clarification of what she meant by that.

Raegan looked off in the direction that Alan had taken. "What Alan is proposing," she explained, then added, "To build a reservoir to divert the water from the Rio Grande to Forever, and to create those irrigation ditches, he needs to funnel the water to where it's needed."

Mike didn't hesitate with his answer. "Right now, Raegan, it seems to be our only viable choice. And because it is," he told her, "I'm all for it. That includes taking part in the building of said reservoir and irrigation ditches." He put his arm around his granddaughter and gave her a quick hug. "We certainly don't lack the man power…or woman power, for that matter," he said tactfully. "And, in my experience, if people feel like they're doing something productive about the situation they find themselves in, they won't spend time brooding about it.

"Instead, they'll feel as if they're doing something to change it—which is a lot more positive than just brooding."

Raegan was in complete agreement. "You're right as always, Grandpa."

Mike Robertson smiled at his granddaughter. Out of all three granddaughters, she was the most like him. Right now, he really felt as if they were on the verge of making some sort of headway, battling this awful drought.

"Just let me know if there's anything I can do to help," he told Raegan. Since she had gone ahead to interact with Alan—a healthy sign, in his point of view—he felt as if he should encourage Raegan to head up the project.

"Thanks, Grandpa. I'll keep that in mind. For now, I'm going to wait until Alan's 'friends' get here so I can evaluate just how serious these people really are about helping to do this work. Once we can get some sort of an idea about how committed these so-called 'altruistic' friends of his are, we can start to get the fundraiser to back the construction costs moving.

"And if you're up for it," Raegan continued, mulling over her grandfather's offer to help, "I think the people in and around Forever would be more receptive to hearing someone like you initiate this fundraiser than listening to someone a lot of them still think of as being a 'whippersnapper,' do it."

"You don't give yourself enough credit, Raegan," her grandfather said. "If you were this so-called 'whippersnapper' you're talking about, you wouldn't have listened to a thing that Alan had to say about the drought, or taken a look at the projections he made. You would have just dismissed his suggestions out of hand," Mike Robertson told his granddaughter.

Raegan pressed her lips together and then shrugged. "I suppose you might have something there."

Mike grinned broadly. "Of course I do. I'm your grandfather. I know everything. Don't you know? I'm older than the hills," he reminded her.

Raegan laughed at the imagery that created in her mind. "Not quite."

"Thank you for that." Mike's eyes crinkled.

"Now come back into the house," he urged her. "I'm sure that your sisters both want to hear what you and 'the hunk,'—their words, not mine— talked about."

Raegan rolled her eyes. "They didn't really call him that, did they?" she asked, as close to horrified as she had been in a long time.

Amused, Mike looked at her. "They're your sisters. You know them a lot better than I do," her grandfather reminded her.

Mike made his way back to the front door and then looked expectantly over his shoulder at her. "Coming?"

It was growing dark. "I guess I'll have to. It's getting late," she noted.

The moment Raegan and her grandfather walked in, Riley and Roe instantly looked in their direction.

"You're back," Riley cried. "We thought that maybe Alan had whisked you away."

"Very funny," Raegan said with a dour expression. "He was showing me the projections for the figures involved in building all these irrigation ditches and that proposed reservoir he feels the town needs."

Roe raised her eyebrows. "Is that all he showed you?" she teased.

"I'll pretend that I didn't hear that," Raegan told her triplet.

"Bet you never thought that Alan White Eagle was ever going to come riding into town to the rescue on a white charger," Riley said.

Raegan blew out a breath. The image her sisters painted were just incredible. It took a lot for her not to make a disparaging comment. "I certainly can't argue with that."

"Oh, sure you could," Riley laughed. "You know that you could argue about *everything*," she told Raegan.

"Girls, girls, girls," Mike called to them before Raegan lost her temper. He could see it coming. "The question now is what you can all do to help and move this along to the sort of conclusion we're all hoping for." Raising an eyebrow, Mike looked from one granddaughter to another. His intention was to make them cease and decease.

"We can all pitch in and help with whatever needs to be done," Riley volunteered, then looked at Raegan. "Right?" she asked.

Deciding to avoid the temptation of saying something sarcastic, Raegan merely replied, "Right."

Rita came into the living room, wiping her

hands on her apron. She had just finished putting all the dishes into the dishwasher and now looked at two of her daughters curiously.

"Are you girls staying the night?" she asked.

Riley shook her head. "I don't know about Roe, but I've got an early morning tomorrow so I'm going to take my leave. Great dinner as always, Mom," Riley told her mother, then turned toward her grandfather. "Great to see you as always, Grandpa," she said. A lopsided smile curved her mouth. "You, too, Rae. Thanks for not killing him," she added, referring to Alan.

"I wouldn't do that to you," Raegan told her sister. "If the sheriff found Alan's dead body here, he'd have to make you testify against me. That would leave Grandpa torn between telling the truth and his loyalty to me." Doing her best to keep a straight face, she looked in her grandfather's direction. "Right, Grandpa?"

"I hereby plead the Fifth," Mike told his oldest granddaughter. Then he glanced at Roe. "How about you, Roe?"

"I definitely wouldn't kill him. I've got better things for that man to do," she told the others with a mischievous glint in her eyes.

"I was asking if you wanted to spend the

night," Mike clarified. "Your old room is still available."

Roe never missed a beat. "Good to know, but I've got to be going, too. It's my turn to open up early for the vet tomorrow," she told the others.

Mike gazed at his granddaughters. There was a great deal of pride in his expression. "You girls all turned out really well."

"Of course they did," Rita agreed. "After all, they have your blood running through their veins," she reminded her father-in-law. "Yours and their father's." The last words were uttered with a trace of wistfulness. "I just wished he was here to see how they turned out."

Mike smiled at his daughter-in-law. "He is, honey. He is. And don't forget, the girls have a great example to follow," he reminded Rita. And then he looked toward Riley and Roe. "All right, girls. Get going. I don't want you to be on the road when it gets really late."

"You wouldn't say that if we were boys," Riley pointed out.

"You're right," Mike agreed. "I wouldn't. So sue me."

Riley and Roe each picked a side and then kissed the man's rough cheeks. "We'd rather kiss you, Grandpa," Riley told him. Then, stepping back, she looked at the other sister who was going to be leaving. "Well, Roe, let's get going. We wouldn't want to worry Grandpa."

He laughed, but quite honestly, he did want them to get on the road. The sooner they did, the sooner they would get home. He pointed toward the door. "Get going, girls."

"Yes, sir," they answered in unison. They paused to kiss the man again, then hugged their mother. "See you soon," they promised, glancing back at Raegan.

"I'm sure you will," Raegan told them. "Alan is coming over for dinner with his friends on Friday, remember?" she reminded her sisters.

She saw her other two sisters' faces suddenly light up. "You're right," Roe told Raegan. "We do have something to live for."

"That all depends on what his friends are like," Riley said.

"Helpful, I hope," Raegan countered. "Otherwise, I'll leave all four of them to you."

Riley's eyes smiled at Raegan. "And here we didn't get you anything."

Their grandfather just laughed and shook his head, thinking, not for the first time, how very empty his life had been until that evening that a very pregnant Rita had turned up on his doorstep... and then everything had instantly brightened.

That Friday, Raegan worked very quickly mucking out the stalls. exercising the horses as well as feeding them. She was determined to get everything finished early before Alan and his engineer friends arrived at the ranch. She even pressed her grandfather's three ranch hands into service in order to help her with the work, something she didn't ordinarily do.

But ranching wasn't the cleanest of endeavors, and she wanted time to grab a quick shower. She wasn't out to impress Alan's friends, but she didn't want to have them turn up their noses at her, either. All she needed was fifteen minutes to herself. Maybe twenty at the most.

Mike Robertson had just walked in himself, when he found he had to step back out of the way to keep from being run over.

"I think that streak that just flew by was your daughter, Rita," he commented. Humor came into his voice. "She certainly is eager to get cleaned up for Alan."

Overhearing him from her place at the top of

the stairs, Raegan called out, "Am not. It's just not polite to come to dinner smelling like sweaty used socks."

Rita inclined her head. "She does have a point."

Mike held up his hands as if surrendering. "I'm not saying anything," he told his daughter-in-law. "Are the other girls coming?" he asked.

Rita looked at him, amused. "What do you think?"

"I think I'm starting to ask foolish questions in my old age," Mike commented.

"You've got at least fifteen more years before you reach 'old age,' Michael Robertson," his daughter-in-law informed him.

"You're lying through those pretty teeth of yours, Rita, but I'm not about to argue with you," Mike chuckled. He looked at the dinner preparations she had spread out over the kitchen counter. "Need any help?" he asked.

"Just the usual," she answered.

He nodded, knowing this response by heart. "Stay out of your way until you're all finished," he answered knowingly.

It was always the same answer, but it still didn't hurt to ask, he thought. One day, Rita might actually decide that she needed a little help.

"Oh, wait, I did just think of something you could do for me," Rita told him.

About to walk out of the kitchen, he turned on his heel. "I'm listening."

"You can answer the door if the doorbell rings before Raegan can come down, if Roe and Riley arrive."

"Oh, they'll be here," he guaranteed his daughter-in-law. "If I know the girls, they'll be here early and salivating."

She laughed as she continued seasoning the pot roast. "They did look pretty interested, didn't they?" she asked, thinking of the expressions on Riley's and Roe's faces.

"That they did," Mike agreed. "They're at that age," he said. "Speaking of interest, I happened to notice that Tom Mastriano has been eyeing you every time you walk into his store."

"The man is just nearsighted," Rita told her father-in-law. "He eyes everyone who crosses his path," Rita pointed out. "Besides," she went on, smiling at Mike, "you're still my 'best' guy, Dad."

"You know, you really are good for my ego," he told her. "Even though I fully expect to see your nose start growing at any moment."

Mike watched Rita carefully flip the pot roast

onto its other side, then season it before putting it back into the oven.

"Well, I think I'll get out of your way," he told her.

Rita looked up for a moment. "Good idea," she agreed with an easy smile.

Walking out of the kitchen, Mike was very nearly run over by Raegan for the second time within the last little while.

"Hey, easy now," he said, catching her by the shoulders. "Don't let him see how eager you are to see him."

Raegan's eyes narrowed. "I am *not* eager, Grandpa," she informed the man. "It's just bad manners to keep someone waiting, that's all." And the last thing she wanted was to hear Alan comment on that if he and his entourage wound up arriving early.

Mike laughed. "Your grandmother could have learned a thing or two from you," he told Raegan. "No matter how much time she had to get ready, that woman was always late."

"Maybe she was just hoping to make you eager to see her," Raegan suggested.

"Oh, that I was," he recalled with nostalgic smile. "That I was." Just then, the doorbell rang.

"Looks like the guests are here ahead of your sisters," he commented, heading for the door.

Out of the corner of his eye, he saw Raegan run her hand through her hair, patting it into place.

Mike smiled to himself as he went to let in his guests.

Chapter Ten

Much as she hated to admit it, since Alan had come to dinner earlier in the week, Raegan had found herself looking forward to today and having Alan come over with his friends. She told herself it was strictly because Alan and his crew of engineering friends represented the only hope that Forever had.

He had already quoted facts and figures to her, but she felt that she wasn't going to be sold on anything until she was able to meet the other engineers who were involved. According to Alan, they were capable engineers and were more than able to get the job done.

Despite the barbs she had tossed his way and what she had flippantly told her family, Raegan found herself believing that Alan could deliver exactly what he said he could.

In the midst of all that, she had to ask herself if she was just being a fool, or if there was something else involved.

For now, she sat quietly at the table, observing and listening while everyone else did the talking.

Her family certainly seemed as if they were willing to believe this group of fresh-faced engineers, and that included Alan among their number.

Her mother, who had always been the outgoing, warm type for as long as Raegan could remember, had immediately welcomed Chris Collins, Logan Walker and Greg Cunningham into her home. And even her grandfather, who was usually somewhat reserved at first, didn't really stand on ceremony when Alan brought in his friends to meet her family. Mike Robertson was almost as welcoming to these engineers as her mother was.

As far as she and her sisters went, there was the usual stunned reaction when Alan's friends walked into her house and had their first encounter with the trio.

"I feel like I'm seeing things," the rather heavyset Greg Cunningham commented as he looked from one triplet to the next. "And I haven't even had my usual glass of wine yet."

"Forgive me for staring," Logan Walker apologized to Raegan and her sisters, "but you ladies really do look incredibly alike. *Really* alike," he emphasized.

"Actually, that's not completely true," Alan interjected, joining them. "Raegan here has a dimple in her right cheek. Her sisters don't," he told his friends. "It doesn't pop up that often because Raegan has to be smiling at the time and that's something she rarely does. But every so often," he concluded with a smile, "it does come up."

"I smile a lot," Raegan protested. "For instance, I smile every time I realize that you're not here."

Chris Collins laughed. "Looks like she's got you there, White Eagle."

Collins might have been a dedicated engineer, but it was obvious that unlike his friend Cunningham, who loved to eat, the blond-haired Collins had a secondary passion that revolved around working out and bodybuilding.

"Everyone, dinner is served," Rita announced, drawing everyone's attention toward the dining-room table. "Please, come in. Sit," she told the group of engineers, as well as her family, as she gestured toward the table. "And, because of Alan, there will be two desserts tonight. Alan's favorite, peach cobbler, and for those who aren't fans of peach cobbler, there is a platter of brownies."

Greg made an appreciative noise. "I might never leave here."

Logan rolled his eyes. "Now you've done it, ma'am," the man confided. "You might think he's kidding, but Cunningham here takes his desserts very seriously."

After sitting down and beginning the meal, Alan glanced around the table as he watched his friends' eating frenzy get underway. "They might not look it now," Alan told Raegan's family, "but when they're not stuffing their faces— and they're doing that because, I can safely say, this has to be the best pot roast any of us have *ever* had…" He paused and nodded his thanks toward Rita. "But these guys are pretty damn good engineers and they can all tell you, I don't toss praise around lightly."

"Are you boys all irrigation engineers, like Alan?" Mike asked.

"For Chris and Logan, being irrigation engineers is a secondary discipline," Alan told his host. "Greg here knows how to build dams and reservoirs. We can all cross over into different disciplines when we need to," he said to Raegan's family sincerely.

Raegan looked at her sisters. Both appeared to be hanging on Alan's every word, as well as what his friends were saying.

As if to prove her right, Riley asked the men, "Where did you all meet?"

"College," Chris answered. "At least that's where Alan, Logan and I met. As for Greg, we ran into him at a fast-food place. He had ordered this huge take-out lunch, then found he had forgotten to bring his wallet with him." The engineer grinned. It was obvious that Chris took great pleasure in telling this story...and not for the first time. "We felt sorry for the big guy and decided to take up a collection to pay his bill, which, since he really loved to eat, was pretty hefty.

"The bill," Chris added, humor playing on his lips, "will finally be all paid off by the end of next month."

Rather than dispute the story, or its origin, Greg just pretended to scowl at his friends, his dark eyebrows forming an extremely shaggy V over the bridge of his nose.

"So I like to eat. Sue me," Greg told his friends.

"There's nothing wrong with having a healthy appetite, Greg," Rita told the young, somewhat robust engineer.

"Mom's right," Raegan said, finally speaking up. "Don't let Alan get to you." She looked at the young man sitting across from her. "When I was a kid, Alan's main hobby at the time was picking fights and making people miserable." She fluttered her lashes at Alan. "Looks like some things don't really ever change."

Alan's eyes drifted over her, from her head down to almost her waist, or at least as far as he could see.

"Oh, I don't know," he said, grinning at her. "It looks like some things actually do."

Raegan could feel the warmth drifting over her, shimmying up and down her spine. What was it about this man? Raegan thought, annoyed at herself for her reaction to the way Alan looked at her. Damn the man, but he had managed to make her blush.

Again.

And this time it was in front of a dining room

full of people, not just him, she thought resentfully.

Time to move this in a new direction, Raegan decided. She looked around at his friends. "Are all of you free tomorrow morning?" she asked.

Chris grinned at her. "Even if we weren't, I think that something could be arranged." He raised an eyebrow. "Just what is it that you have in mind?"

"Well, I thought we could all go to see Eric Harrigan," Raegan began.

Greg looked up from his meal. "Who's that?" he asked.

"He's the man who runs Forever's hotel. If we can make him understand what you all intend to do to end the drought and bring much-needed water to Forever, and, moreover, that you're not planning on soaking the residents doing it—you should only pardon the expression—I am sure that Mr. Harrigan would be willing to put you boys up at the hotel at what would amount to cost."

Logan was more than happy to entertain that proposition. "That sounds good to me. What about you, Alan?" his friend asked. "Are you planning on staying at the hotel, too?"

Alan nodded. "I figure it's actually a good idea," he said to his friends. "If we're all under the same roof, it's a lot simpler and will cut down on the time it takes to go back and forth. Besides, if something occurs to any of us about all this, all we'll have to do is just walk down the hall."

"You mean you," Greg said in between taking healthy-sized bites of his meal. His broad smile reflected his pleasure.

Alan's mouth curved. "Yeah, I guess I do," he admitted. Then he looked around at his friends. "So what do you say? Are you up for staying in Forever's hotel?"

"Hey, as long as it's free, or close to free," Chris said, glancing in Raegan's direction, "count me in."

"I'll do what I can," Raegan promised.

"Miss Joan will want to show the town's gratitude by feeding all of you a few times a week," Riley told them, wanting to contribute to the conversation.

"Miss Joan?" Logan repeated quizzically. He was obviously unfamiliar with the name.

"She's the town's unofficial fairy godmother," Roe told Alan's engineer friends.

"Miss Joan owns the diner," Mike explained, thinking a little more information might be needed to complete the picture. "She's been in

Forever since the town came into existence…or practically that long."

"She likes to act gruff, but the woman has just about the biggest heart humanly possible," Raegan informed the others at the table.

"I can definitely second that," Riley told Alan's friends. "The first time I ever saw her, I must have been around three and I thought she was the scariest human being on the face of the earth. But eventually, I realized that she was really a nice person. I know that she's going to want to find a way to pay all of you back for your time and your efforts."

"Will you be coming along?" Logan asked, looking Riley.

"You want someone to hold your hand?" Alan asked, amused.

"Hey, that sounds pretty good to me," the young engineer said. "As long as it's not your hand I'm holding, Alan," Logan concluded, then smiled at Riley.

Alan laughed. "You don't have to worry about that." He looked pointedly around the table at the faces of his friends. "Did you guys get a chance to look at the figures involved for the proposal I left with you?"

"I did," Greg said, speaking up as he finished

his second helping of pot roast and eyed a third. "I've got a few suggestions and questions."

Alan nodded, pleased. "Good, good," he commented. "That means once we stop at the hotel and then pay Miss Joan a visit, we can get right down to business," he said, then looked at Raegan. "Sound right to you, Raegan?"

She was surprised that he had actually consulted her on this. It looked as if this was going to work out after all, she decided.

Raegan slanted a look toward her grandfather and could tell by the expression on his face that the older man looked pleased about this turn of events, too.

Leave it to that man to be one step ahead of her, Raegan thought. But then, Mike Robertson had always been able to see the good in people.

Out of nowhere, she suddenly felt bad that her grandfather and father had spent so many years clashing with one another instead of finding a way to get along.

"Where are you boys staying tonight?" Mike asked suddenly.

"Alan's cousins are putting us up for the night and then we'll go to the hotel, the way we planned on doing even before Raegan here came up with the idea of bargaining with the guy who runs the place," Chris explained.

Rita exchanged looks with her father-in-law. After all these years together, she could easily guess what was on his mind. It also helped that they thought alike.

"We have plenty of room here," Rita told the four engineers. "You can all spend the night here," she said. "That way you boys can continue talking about those plans that Alan wrote up, and then tomorrow, you can collect your things from the White Eagle horse ranch and go on to the hotel."

"We wouldn't want to put you out, Mrs. Robertson," Logan protested.

"The way all of us see it, we're the ones putting you boys out. After all, we're taking advantage of your generosity and your engineering expertise." Rita glanced in her father-in-law's direction. "What do you say, Dad?"

"Honestly, I can't see these boys turning down such a generous offer, but ultimately, it's not up to me." Mike looked at his granddaughters. "How about it, girls? You agree with your mother?"

"Absolutely," Roe told her grandfather.

"Makes a lot of sense to me. There are two

extra bedrooms now that Roe and I moved out. The beds are extra large. Each bed is big enough for two big, strong, strapping guys," Riley told Alan's friends.

"What do you say, guys?" Alan asked his friends.

"Depends on what Raegan thinks," Chris said, looking at her.

Raegan looked at the engineer in surprise. "Me?" she asked. "What do I have to do with it?"

"Well, Alan here seemed to indicate that you're the one who's running the show. After all, you're the one who suggested the negotiations for the hotel rooms and you also came up with the idea of the diner owner giving us free food, or close to free food. So as far as we're concerned, you're running this show. Are we wrong?" Chris asked.

"No, you weren't wrong," Mike told the young man. "Raegan is always full of a lot of good ideas. She just doesn't realize that she has a habit of orchestrating things and telling people what to do. But always with the best of intentions," her grandfather added. "But if the idea of staying here for the night makes any of you uncomfortable, you shouldn't feel as if you are obligated to stay," the man told them in all seriousness. "Just make sure that you swing by here for breakfast tomorrow morning before you boys start your day."

"Mrs. Robertson?" Alan said, turning toward Raegan's mother. "Will that be all right with you?"

Rita beamed, although she was surprised that Alan had thought to even put that question to her. "That's just perfect with me, Alan. I look forward to it."

"Then we'll see you all here tomorrow morning," Mike said, shaking each engineer's hand as the young men all filed out of his house, one by one.

Chapter Eleven

Eric Harrigan appeared to be deeply involved with reviewing the various stacks of paperwork that went with running the hotel.

When Raegan arrived in Eric's office with Alan and his friends, the hotel manager was taken aback at first. Pushing aside the vast piles of paperwork, he scanned the faces of the four men that Raegan had brought in behind her. Harrigan seemed to vaguely recognize Alan from the town-hall meeting, but not the others.

"How can I help you gentlemen?" he asked politely after he nodded at Raegan. "If you're here, I am assuming that you will be needing rooms for your stay in Forever."

"Oh, yes, they definitely will," Raegan assured him.

Aside from being hotel manager, Eric Harrigan was also part owner of the hotel. His partner in the hotel was Constance Carmichael Murphy, who had overseen the hotel's initial construction. She was also married to one of the Murphy brothers, the one who ran the local saloon.

Raegan took over the introductions. "This is Chris Collins, Logan Walker and Greg Cunningham, the engineers who volunteered to help Alan bring water to our severely parched ranches and farms. Guys, this is Eric Harrigan, the hotel's manager and part owner.

"Miss Joan thought," Raegan continued, conveniently dropping the unofficial town matriarch's name to help sell Harrigan on the idea she was promoting, since no one ever said no to the woman, "that in exchange for their help, you would be willing to put them up in your hotel at cost."

Harrigan looked from one face to another, clearly caught off guard by this turn of events. "When you say these gentlemen are volunteering…" He allowed his voice to trail off, waiting for Raegan or Alan to fill in the empty space and confirm what they actually meant by the word *volunteering*.

Alan tore his eyes away from Raegan, impressed with the way the girl he had once thought of as a pain in the neck had managed to take over,, advancing their cause all while looking absolutely delectable.

"None of us are charging the town for our time," Alan informed the hotel manager. "Only for the materials that will be used to construct the various irrigation ditches. Also to build the new reservoir that'll contain the water being redirected from the Rio Grande."

The hotel manager appeared somewhat skeptical. "It's not that I don't trust you boys, but will I get a chance to look at this paperwork?"

Raegan knew she was taking liberties, but sometimes, that was necessary.

"Absolutely," she said with conviction. "This is all going to be aboveboard every step of the way," she promised Harrigan. "I am preparing to hold a fundraiser in order to cover the cost of all the materials that are going to be used in this construction."

"And my part in all this is just to provide the hotel rooms for these 'saviors' of Forever?" Harrigan asked, curious. He looked from Raegan to Alan.

The hotel manager was a fairly recent transplant to Forever, having moved here just after the hotel had been completed. He had never met Alan before the latter had appeared at the townhall meeting several days ago. He had to admit that Alan had a persuasive manner about him, but at the time he hadn't been a 100 percent sold on the proposition.

However, since this edict was coming from Miss Joan, Harrigan saw no reason why he couldn't join in and do his part in all of this.

"All right," Harrigan finally decided, nodding his head. "Count me in." And then he seemed a little leery as he glanced at the faces of the engineers. "You do understand that the hotel will be providing you with rooms and not suites?" he asked.

"Oh, rooms will be more than adequate," Alan responded. "We just need a place to lay our heads at night and a place to confer once the day winds down."

"That is definitely doable," Harrigan confirmed, reaching into a drawer and scooping up four separate key cards. He programmed numbers into each of the cards, then distributed them to the engineers.

"There you go, gentlemen. The modern equivalent of room keys. Am I the first one on board with this?" he asked, looking toward Raegan.

She smiled at the man. "The very first one," Raegan answered. "That is, if you don't count Miss Joan."

For the first time, Harrigan actually smiled. "We all make it a point to *always* count Miss Joan."

"We'll be holding another town meeting late on Sunday afternoon," Alan told the hotel manager. "What do you say, guys?" he asked, looking at his friends. "Does tomorrow afternoon to review my calculations work for you, or is that too soon?"

"I think the sooner you can get this out on the table and start working toward the end goal, the faster I can get the fundraiser going," Raegan told Alan.

"Fundraiser?" Harrigan echoed. For a moment, he had forgotten that Raegan had talked about that being a way to raise the extra money that would be needed.

Raegan nodded. "Well, yes. These engineers are donating their time, but the materials that are going to be necessary for this aren't going to be free. Each engineer here has friends who know friends who might be able to swing excellent prices for the items involved, but there are still going to be some large price tags involved," she told the hotel manager.

Harrigan thought about this new turn of events. "You have a location in mind for this fundraiser you want to hold?" he asked. "The room that we use for weddings and receptions isn't booked at the moment," Harrigan offered.

Raegan knew where he was going with this and her thoughts were leaning in a different direction.

"That's very generous of you," Raegan told the man, "but I was thinking more along the lines of Miss Joan's diner." She had a very good reason for this. "One look from that woman will have the residents of Forever digging deep into their pockets faster than anything any one of us can accomplish."

Harrigan saw no reason to argue against taking that path. "You're probably right. I can't picture anyone saying 'no' to Miss Joan. Not if they plan to eat out ever again," he said with a laugh. Looking at Alan and his friends, he told them, "Feel free to move into your rooms at any time.

I'll have the maid get those rooms ready for you within the hour, and I look forward to seeing you at the town-hall meeting to hear you flesh out those plans of yours."

"So, next stop Miss Joan's diner?" Alan asked Raegan.

"That's what we agreed on. I take it that you could all probably stand to have something to eat," Raegan asked, looking at Alan's friends.

"I don't know about the others, but I could sure stand to have something to eat," Greg told Raegan wistfully.

Logan glanced at his friend, humor curving his generous mouth. "You can *always* stand to get something to eat."

Greg responded the way his father had taught him to answer when he was much younger, even though this was far less true now than it had been at the time. "Hey, I'm a growing boy."

Chris shook his head in amazement. "You 'grow' any more and they might have to reinforce the floor at the town-hall center."

"Okay, guys, playtime is over," Alan declared. "You need to put on your serious faces before I take you to meet Miss Joan for the first time. Your job is to impress her, not make the woman roll those penetrating hazel eyes of hers. Am I right, Raegan?" Alan asked, suddenly turning and putting the question to Raegan.

Raegan found herself practically speechless as she looked at him in surprise. "Miss Joan feels that humor has its place, but the drought has made everyone far more serious than they're comfortable about. Being the way she is about Forever, I know that Miss Joan feels all this personally."

"I think that everyone does," Alan told Raegan. "All right, let's go," he urged the group, then looked at Raegan. "You can come in the truck with us if you'd rather not have to drive to the diner."

"That's all right, I'll meet you there," she told him. "Your truck only has so much space to spare and I don't relish the idea of being crushed up against you."

Alan grinned at her, although he did lower his voice. "Funny, I do."

Raegan lowered her own voice as well. "In your dreams, White Eagle."

"As a matter of fact, yes," he told Raegan.

For the life of her, Raegan wasn't able to come up with a flippant retort to put Alan in his place, or actually any sort of retort at all.

Once again, with just a well-aimed, sexy look, Alan had managed to send a warm, rather unnerving shiver and have it go slithering up and down her spine. Along the way, a whole host of butterflies were released throughout her shaky system.

"I'll meet you at the diner," she told him, walking out of the hotel lobby.

Miss Joan looked instantly alert the moment that Raegan walked into the diner.

Raegan had to admit that the woman's rarely seen smile began to spread the moment that Miss Joan looked over her head and focused on the four young men walking in directly behind her.

Nodding at Raegan and Alan, Miss Joan asked them, "Who are your friends?"

Raegan glanced in Alan's direction. Since the three engineers were his friends, not hers, Raegan decided it best to leave the introductions up to him.

Alan found himself picking up on what she was thinking immediately, surprised at how easily he could read Raegan.

Maybe there was something more going on here than he had thought.

"Miss Joan," he said, indicating the three engineers, "I'd like you to meet my friends, Chris Collins, Logan Walker and Greg Cunningham. They're here to lend me the benefit of their expertise and help me bring water to Forever so we can attempt to revitalize the ranches and farms within the area," Alan said to the owner of the diner.

Miss Joan thought back to the meeting Alan had led several days ago. She looked at him, somewhat impressed.

"Well, that didn't take you very long to arrange, did it?" she asked, looking over each engineer in turn. She was pleased to note that none of them shifted uncomfortably. That was a good sign, the woman thought.

"Welcome, boys," she said, greeting the three other engineers. "We could certainly use your help—not that I don't think that Alan here could handle this on his own in the long run, but the problem is, we might not *have* a long run. So what can I get you boys?" she asked, then added, "Order anything you like. It's on the house."

"They haven't had lunch yet," Raegan volunteered. She saw Miss Joan glance at her wristwatch and guessed what the woman had to be thinking. "They wanted to settle into the hotel first."

Miss Joan nodded. "Then lunch it is," she announced. "Just tell Alicia what you'd like," the diner owner said, indicating the server who had just come up to join her.

Alan leaned in toward Raegan. "I don't remember seeing Miss Joan being this friendly and outgoing."

He heard Raegan stifle a laugh. "Don't question it," she told Alan. "Just be glad it's happening."

"Oh, I am. Trust me, I am," Alan told her with no small show of enthusiasm.

There was a twinkle in his eyes again, Raegan couldn't help noting. Had it always been that way and she just hadn't noticed? Raegan wondered, because she certainly could not remember seeing that almost hypnotic sparkle in Alan's eyes every time he turned them in her direction.

Focus, Raegan, she told herself. This was no time to have PG-rated thoughts about Alan.

Meanwhile, the server was busy taking down the engineers' lunch orders. Deciding to keep them company, at least in theory, Raegan ordered a cup of coffee.

Everything arrived in record time and all of

the engineers, including Alan, began eating their lunches with gusto.

Miss Joan returned in ten minutes to see if everything met with the engineers' satisfaction. "How is everything?" the woman asked, sounding unusually diplomatic for Miss Joan, Raegan observed.

Since everyone else's mouth was full, Raegan decided to take the lead. "Everything is just great," she answered.

Miss Joan's eyes narrowed as she looked at Raegan. "You're just drinking coffee, girl," the woman pointed out.

"Yes," Raegan agreed. "And they're the ones who are eating," she said, nodding at the four men. "But I know enthusiasm when I see it."

Miss Joan looked around at the occupants of the table. She smiled, pleased. "Yes, so do I," she replied. "I'll leave you to enjoy your meals, boys, and when you're done, we'll talk," the woman promised.

True to her word, Miss Joan returned just as a busboy was gathering up the empty plates. Feeling compelled to be the perfect hostess, she asked, "How was everything?"

"Terrific as always, Miss Joan," Alan responded.

His sentiment was echoed by all three of his friends.

"All right, now that your stomachs are full, have you reached any conclusions as to what your course of action is going to be?" the diner owner asked, looking at each engineer carefully, ending with Alan.

"Yes, ma'am, we have," Alan answered her. "We'll be outlining everything at the town-hall meeting tomorrow."

"So you do have a plan?" Miss Joan asked.

"Yes, ma'am, we do. We'll be donating our time and Raegan here is going to initiate a fund-raiser so that money can be raised to cover all the expenses that will be needed to get all the materials that will be necessary to carry out these plans."

The sooner she got this out, the better, Raegan thought. "We're hoping to be able to use your diner for the fundraiser," Raegan told the woman.

To her surprise, her words were actually met with a smile from Miss Joan.

"That," Miss Joan declared, "is an excellent idea. And to launch it, why don't we have a get-acquainted party at Murphy's Saloon the day after the town-hall meeting?"

It was a suggestion, but being Miss Joan, she didn't anticipate any opposition.

And she didn't get any.

Chapter Twelve

Alan and the other engineers spent the rest of the day as well as part of the next morning reviewing the facts and the figures that Alan had come up with. In addition, they prepared to deliver the simplest of outlines as to what they intended to do about tackling and fixing the water situation.

Anything more complex, Alan reasoned, and he was afraid that he might lose at least half of his audience, if not more. If the people in the audience had more specific questions to ask, they would be addressed on a more private basis.

As it turned out, the summation that Alan and his friends wound up delivering at the town-hall meeting was an even more in-depth review of what he had previously extrapolated on when he had addressed them on his own.

By the time Alan and his friends had finished taking turns and speaking, the audience sitting in the meeting hall initially met the news with complete silence.

Forever's residents sat looking at one another as if they didn't know what to make of what they were being told.

And then Randall James, one of Forever's older residents, raised his hand and spoke up. "This all sounds like it's going to cost a lot of money," he said to Alan in what could only be taken as an accusatory voice.

"Well, I won't lie," Alan told the rancher. "This sort of thing doesn't come cheap, but—"

"Look," Randall said, annoyed as he cut in on Alan's answer. "I guess you probably mean well, but we've all weathered dry summers here before and we've all survived. No reason to think this is going to be any different. We don't want to spend all this money, building some damn reservoir and putting in a bunch of irrigation ditches just because there's a little dry spell going on," the senior rancher said.

Miss Joan, sitting in the front row, turned around in her seat and pinned the rancher with a far-from-benevolent look. "And what if this 'dry spell' winds up lasting through the late fall, or longer? Are you willing to lose your ranch and the ranches of all of your friends, no matter how small a number that might be?" she added with a touch of sarcasm. "Seems like that would be a pretty big risk to me."

"So where are we supposed to come up with all this money?" James asked, staring hard at Alan and the other engineers. "This isn't a rich town."

"If you've been listening, Mr. James, instead of getting all up in arms," Raegan said, speaking up, "you would have heard that Alan and his friends plan to hold a fundraiser to raise the money for the materials they'll be needing. And, as I recall, the residents of Forever have never been afraid of getting a little dirt under their nails by pitching in to work right next to their neighbors," she pointedly reminded the rancher, her eyes flashing.

Lord, but Raegan was magnificent when she got her back up and had fire in her eyes, Alan couldn't help thinking. He found himself being really drawn to her.

"Hell, I don't need to be preached to by a little slip of a thing," the disgruntled rancher said angrily.

Alan was about to put the man in his place, but before he or anyone else realized it, Miss Joan had risen to her feet, drawing herself up like a powerful force.

Her eyes blazing, Miss Joan asked, "Would you rather I did the preaching, Randall?" she asked. "Let's say you're right and this drought passes before Forever finds itself completely high and dry and about to go up like a tinderbox. With the ditches dug and the reservoir built, we'll be ready when the next threat shows up on our doorstep—and make no mistake about it, there *will* be one.

"But if the drought continues," Miss Joan went on, "and we haven't taken the necessary precautions, everyone in and around Forever stands to lose their ranches and their farms." Her eyes narrowed. "Are you willing to have that happen?"

The rancher shifted uncomfortably. "No, of course not, but I—"

"Then shut up and stop arguing, Randall,"

Miss Joan snapped. She looked over toward Alan and the other engineers. "Anyone else have something to add?" she asked, scanning the rest of the meeting hall.

Alan shook his head, smiling gratefully at the woman. "Can't think of a thing, Miss Joan. You've said everything that needed to be said."

Miss Joan nodded her head, satisfied. "Fine, then. I want all of you to know that you are invited over to Murphy's Saloon tomorrow at six to officially kick off the fundraiser. First round of drinks will be on Harry and me," she told the crowd, nodding toward her husband. "The rest will be your responsibility." And then she looked back at the rancher who had raised his objections to Alan's proposal. "That all right with you, Randall?"

The man inclined his head. It was obvious that, not having a death wish, he was not about to oppose Miss Joan twice in one day. "Yes, ma'am."

She nodded her head. "Good, then unless you or anyone else has anything else to add—" Miss Joan looked around at the people at the meeting. "No? Then I hereby call this meeting officially adjourned."

Miss Joan hadn't opened the meeting so it

really was not up to her to adjourn it, Raegan thought, but she knew that no one was about to point that out to the woman.

"See you all tomorrow at Murphy's Saloon," Miss Joan told the attendees.

As everyone filed out of the town meeting, Raegan saw the rather bemused expression on Alan's face as he stood out of the way and watched the people leave.

"What?" she finally asked the engineer.

"Just thinking that if Miss Joan was in charge of running the world, we might actually live to see world peace restored," Alan mused.

Raegan watched as several people paused by the collection box that had been set up by the exit. They tossed in a few bills before they left the meeting hall.

"I have no doubt of that," Raegan commented. She watched as the last of the people filed out. "I had better get this to Miss Joan," she said, picking up the box. "I know she wants to oversee this collection being taken up at the diner. I get the distinct impression that she believes people will be more inclined to make donations in her presence than just haphazardly tossing money into the box when no one is looking."

Alan agreed. "I'll walk you to the car," he offered. Then, looking over toward the other engineers, he told them, "I'll meet you later at the hotel." With that, he took hold of the collection box, his intent clear.

"I can handle this," Raegan told him as she reached to take possession of the box again. "This isn't exactly heavy." To prove her point, she hefted the collection box. Raegan had nothing against politeness, but she hated being regarded as helpless.

Undeterred, Alan's eyes met hers. "I know," he replied.

Raegan could feel herself beginning to smile. "Suit yourself," she told him, releasing her hold on the box.

Alan's response completely threw her. Nodding his head, he answered, "Only with your permission, Raegan."

Raegan had no idea what to make of that, but she decided that for her own peace of mind, now was not the time to attempt to speculate as to what he was trying to say.

When Raegan and Alan walked in with the collection box, Miss Joan looked as if she had been expecting them. "I was wondering which one of you would bring this to the diner." The woman smiled at them, pleased. "What took you so long?" she asked.

Raegan's brow furrowed. "Was this supposed to be a test?"

Rather than bristle, Miss Joan just smiled. "Maybe."

Alan just went along with what the woman was saying. "Did we win?" he asked, obviously amused.

Hazel eyes washed over them, and Alan couldn't begin to guess what was going through the woman's mind.

"That still remains to be seen," Miss Joan replied.

"What do you think she meant by that?" Alan asked Raegan after they left the collection box with Miss Joan and walked out of the diner again.

Raegan shook her head. "With Miss Joan, you can never really be sure," she answered.

Alan laughed to himself. "I seem to vaguely recall that," he responded. "Nice to know that some things don't change." Having walked her to her vehicle, he stopped at the driver's side. He found himself reluctant to see her leave. "Will I see you at the party tomorrow?"

"Well, it's a get-acquainted party and you and I have been acquainted for a very long time," she reminded him.

"But not in our present state," Alan pointed out.

She frowned at him, doing her best to ignore the tightening feeling in the pit of her stomach. What was wrong with her anyway? "English, Alan. Speak English."

"You can't pretend that you haven't changed," he told her. "I know I have."

"So now you're Alan 2.0?" Raegan asked, humor entering her eyes.

He took no offense at her choice of words. "Something like that. And if you don't come, Miss Joan will think that I had something to do with chasing you off. She might even have me come and get you." He looked at her. "You wouldn't want that, would you?"

"You've made your point," Raegan told him. "I'll be there."

Alan smiled. The expression on his face did more to unnerve her than anything he could have said.

Starting up her car, Raegan silently called herself an idiot as she drove away.

* * *

Rather than meeting the rest of the family at Murphy's, her sisters came to their grandfather's house first.

"Roe thought that we could all arrive together as a family," Riley explained once she and Roe walked in. Turning around for Raegan's perusal, she held out her dress and asked, "So what do you think?"

It was her grandfather who answered first. "I still think of the three of you as a triple threat." Mike chuckled. "So much beauty all in one place."

Raegan laughed. "The reason none of us are married, Grandpa, is because we could never find anyone to compete with you."

"Well, I would never want you to rush in to anything," Mike Robertson told his granddaughters. "But I'm sure when the right man comes along, you will know it." His eyes swept over all three of his granddaughters. "All of you," he vowed.

"Rita, the girls are all here," Mike announced, calling up the stairs. "Time for us to get going." He turned back to Riley and Roe. "You girls want to drive there in your cars, or come with us?"

"Well, since Riley and I live in town and can walk home once the party is over, we'll just drive back in our vehicles," Roe said, speaking for both of them.

"I'll come with you and Mom," Raegan told her grandfather.

Mike nodded. "Two beautiful women instead of four. I think I can deal with that," he said whimsically. "All right, girls, pile in to the car," he told his daughter-in-law and granddaughter. Glancing toward his other two granddaughters, he told them, "We'll meet you there."

"Sounds good to me, Grandpa," Roe answered. She looked over toward Riley. "Ready?"

Riley grinned mischievously. "I was born ready."

"I'd be careful who I said that around," Raegan warned, thinking of the way that Alan would respond to that declaration.

Although they were fairly early, the party at Murphy's looked to already be in full swing. Because of the unusually warm weather, and the number of people attending, there were tables placed outside of the establishment, as well as the ones inside, in order to provide snacks, courtesy of Miss Joan and the people who worked for her. No one ever went hungry at one of these gatherings.

Liam Murphy and the two other members of his band, Forever's resident musicians, were there to provide music for the gathering.

Despite how crowded Murphy's already was, Alan spotted Raegan the moment that she, her mother and grandfather walked into the establishment.

He quickly made his way over to the family before the crowd grew any larger.

Nodding at the rest of her family by way of welcome, Alan obviously kept his attention focused on Raegan.

His smile was wide and warm as he happily declared, "You made it."

"But I already said that we would come," Raegan pointed out. "Why would you think that we wouldn't?"

She was challenging him and he did his best to give her an answer he felt that she would find acceptable. "Well, you've already done a great deal to move this project along on several fronts. I thought that maybe you'd just kick back and decide to take a break."

Raegan looked at the engineer as if he was just talking nonsense. "None of us can afford to take a break right now, not with this drought hovering over us, getting worse and more pronounced by the day. If I can help get all of this moving in the right direction, I fully intend to." And then she smiled. "Just because you're in charge of this project doesn't mean I'm about to throw up my hands and just walk away."

Even though you might like it that way, Raegan added silently.

"Nice to know I can count on you," Alan told her. "But then, deep down," he continued, his eyes washing over her, "I always knew I could."

When had this change happened—or had he always really been like this and she just hadn't noticed? No matter. She was willing to give him the benefit of the doubt. "Was this before or after you would torture me and call me names?" she asked.

Alan never missed a beat. "After." Switching topics, he redirected Raegan's attention toward the collection box. "Everyone who's come here so far makes a point of stopping at the collection box. If this keeps up, getting those supplies we're going to need to create the ditches and build the reservoir won't be a problem."

"That was the thinking behind having Miss Joan set it up," she reminded Alan.

Just then, she heard Liam's band begin to play. It was a familiar, cheerful number.

"All this and music, too," Alan commented wryly. And then he looked at Raegan. "May I have this dance?" he asked.

His politely worded request caught her off guard. It took her a second to respond. She didn't want to appear too eager. It could still work against her. "Maybe later."

He had no intention of dropping the matter. "As I recall, Raegan, you were very light on your feet."

Raegan looked at him, clearly surprised. She had never danced with him. "How would you know that?"

"Oh, I have my ways," he answered, and then a light came into his eyes as he smiled at her. "Want to prove me wrong?" he asked.

Before she could answer, she felt his arm slip around her waist as he took her hand in his.

The next moment, they were dancing to an old familiar country song as if they had been doing it forever.

Chapter Thirteen

Alan spun her around on the floor, executing more and more intricate moves with each passing moment. And as he did so, he looked increasingly impressed that she was able to keep up.

"I see you've learned how to dance exceptionally well since I was in Forever the last time," he commented to Raegan.

She braced herself for a critical remark to follow on the heels of his compliment, but to her surprise, there wasn't any. The compliment stood on its own.

Still, Raegan felt that if she allowed her guard to go down, she would be leaving herself wide open for some sort of hurtful statement when she least expected it,

In the interest of a potential truce, Raegan decided to attempt to ride out the moment...until such time as Alan wound up proving her wrong.

Little by little Raegan forced herself to relax, at least to some degree. She told herself that she was doing this for Forever's benefit. One way or another, she was not the one who counted here. The people who counted in this matter were the residents of Forever. The residents and their ranches and their farms.

However, if for some reason, he wound up misrepresenting his intent, or deceiving all these people who meant so much to her, she would find a way to essentially make him pay, Raegan promised herself as she continued dancing with Alan.

Although Alan would have preferred to dance closer to the woman he was holding in his arms, the song that the band was playing didn't really encourage it.

Moreover, when the song ended and he drew back, Alan could all but see the serious thoughts that were traveling through her head.

What was that all about? he couldn't help wondering.

"Is there anything wrong?" he finally asked Raegan.

She waved her hand at his question. "I'm just thinking," she replied vaguely.

For some reason, Alan felt as if he had just been put on notice. "Ordinarily, I would say that was a good thing. But right now, I have to admit that I'm not so sure."

What she had been thinking about was whether or not he would ultimately come through for the townspeople. But she knew that sounded antagonistic on her part, so she just allowed him to fill in the blanks however he saw fit.

"Go on," Raegan encouraged warily.

"You know that old-fashioned superstition when you feet a cold shiver go up and down your spine and your grandmother would say that was because death had just jumped over your grave?"

Another song had started up and she continued dancing, mystified as she stared at him. "No, I'm not familiar with that saying, but I'll take your word for it."

"Well, anyway," he continued, "that's kind of the way I feel, as if death had just jumped over my grave."

She stared at him, doing her best to connect

the dots. "Is that your subtle way of evaluating dancing with me?"

He laughed, somewhat stunned. "No," he said without any hesitation. "If anything, that shiver I just described going up and down my spine was meant to be a compliment paid to you."

At that point, the song ended, but she remained standing where she was, doing her best to make sense out of the situation she found herself in.

And then it suddenly hit her. Raegan cocked her head. "Are you flirting with me?"

"Maybe," Alan replied. His eyes met hers. "How am I doing?"

She was completely stunned. "You take my breath away, I'll give you that."

His smile widened. "That's a good thing, right?"

Raegan felt as if his smile was caressing her. She laughed at his response. "Only you could have asked that."

"That's what makes me unique," he told her with a wink.

The band began playing yet another rousing number. Alan continued holding her against him. "Are you up to having yet another dance?" he asked Raegan.

There it was again, that hypnotic look in his eyes, taking and holding her prisoner. Even as she contemplated pushing Alan away for form's sake, there was something going on within her chest that stopped her.

Something that definitely warmed up to him. That warmed up to the look in his eyes.

"Sure, why not?" Raegan finally answered gamely, doing her best to sound nonchalant and completely unaffected by the close proximity of the man who was holding her, even if the reality of the situation was anything but.

Alan's response was to smile at her and that just sent her pulse going up even higher. Raegan found that it was increasingly more difficult for her to catch her breath.

When the song that the band was playing had finished, Raegan was all set to withdraw her hand from Alan's and step away. However, the next song the band struck up was even more familiar and it was one that was far much slower in tempo.

"Just one more?" Alan asked. He added, "For old time's sake?"

"For old time's sake?" she echoed. "That would indicate that at one point or another, we actually danced to this song." And she knew for a fact that they hadn't. They had never danced to any song.

"Pretend we did," he told her, a smile playing on his lips. "At least just for the next three minutes."

Raegan knew that if she raised a fuss, Alan would back off. But for reasons she didn't quite understand, she really didn't want that to happen. If she was being completely honest with herself, Raegan would have to admit that she didn't find dancing with Alan like this exactly off-putting.

If anything, the exact opposite was true.

But just as she found herself warming to this rare moment, some of the ranchers came up to them, apologizing for the interruption. What they wanted to do was thank Alan for what he and his friends were about to do for the town.

Walt Sheldon, one of the older farmers, put the residents' gratitude into more practical terms. "I hear that you're going to need some man power to help dig those ditches. My friends and I would like to volunteer to do that when the time comes."

Alan appreciated the offer and was actually counting on the help when the time came. But he wanted these people to know exactly what they were signing up for.

"It's going to come faster than you think," Alan warned.

Walt flashed a toothy grin. "Fine with us. Just let us know when and where and we'll be there. You and your friends—" Walt waved his hand around the bar room, indicating the three other engineers "—have given us hope, boy. The least we can do is give you the benefit of our muscle."

"My friends and I appreciate that," Alan told the farmer. "As soon as we have the groundwork laid out in more detail, we'll be sure to be in touch with you."

The farmer nodded. "I'll let everyone else know," Walt replied. "We'll be waiting to hear from you."

Raegan waited until Walt and his friends withdrew and went back to the celebration to say something. "It looks like you're the man of the hour," she told Alan.

"Not just me," he corrected. "All of us. We're all going to have to pull together in order to get this off the ground."

"By 'we' you're referring to your engineer friends," Raegan said, making an assumption.

"Yes, them," Alan agreed. "But not just them. I'm including as many of the people in town as are willing to do the work, because the more of them that we can get to help with the digging, the less money we'll need to spend on bringing in outside contractors." He saw the smile bloom on Raegan's face. Knowing he hadn't said anything humorous, he led her over to the side and asked, "What?"

"Who would have ever known that that kid I dreaded seeing every summer would have turned out to be such a huge asset to Forever," Raegan admitted, marveling at the thought.

"Really?" Alan asked her in surprise. "You actually dreaded seeing me every summer?"

Raegan nodded. "You have no idea," she told him, thinking back to those days.

"I guess I don't," he allowed. He supposed he had suspected it to a degree, but he had never actually been sure of that. "And how do you feel about me now?" Alan asked, looking at her.

"The jury's still out on that," she answered vaguely. And then, because of the situation, she felt compelled to clarify. "But at least you seem to be making progress in the right direction. But how can you afford to do all this on a volunteer basis?" she asked. "For that matter, how can your friends afford to undertake this for free?"

"I don't do everything for free," he told her. "I do take on some paying jobs. But my parents did leave me a sizable inheritance—probably to make up for ignoring me most of my childhood—and that allows me to be able to pick and choose the causes I do want to undertake. Not to mention that Miss Joan has that collection going, so that the expenses that do wind up arising will be covered. Between that and the volunteer labor, this whole project should all go rather smoothly," he told her. "Or at least as smoothly as something of this magnitude can go."

"Well, I certainly hope that you're right," Raegan said.

Alan noted that a lot of the people attending this party Miss Joan and the Murphy brothers had thrown were now walking by carrying plates of food they had helped themselves to.

"You want to get something to eat before there's nothing left?" he suggested.

"Sure." She laughed as she and Alan approached one of several tables that were strategically placed in the premises. "This certainly is a hungry crowd," she agreed. "They're probably anticipating all the work they're going to have to be doing soon and are storing up the food to provide them with energy," Raegan wryly noted.

Alan watched as Raegan put a few things on

her plate. In his judgment, there appeared to hardly be anything there.

"Is that all you're eating?" he asked her incredulously.

She smiled. "I've always found that a little goes a long way."

He nodded, but found himself getting lost in her eyes and struggled to pull himself out. "That just applies to food, right?" he said more to himself than to her.

She heard him nonetheless, but decided not to comment.

Looking around the immediate area, she saw that there wasn't any available place for them to sit.

"Want to go outside?" he suggested. "It looks like there's still seating out there."

It was getting dark outside, even though there was light coming from within Murphy's. The accompanying music added a measure of warmth to the scene despite the growing darkness.

After a moment's hesitation, she answered. "Sure, why not?" she agreed, walking out next to Alan.

Gazing around, he found a space for them and gestured toward the table. Raegan slid in and proceeded to begin to eat the small plate of food she had carried out with her.

"Tell me something. Just between you and me, do you have any regrets about coming in and undertaking this project?" she asked, looking at him closely. She felt rather sure that she could see through him if he attempted to snow her.

"Actually, no. If I had any second thoughts, I wouldn't have agreed to come," he told her. "Like I said when I came over to your grandfather's house last week, Forever was and is like my second home. Actually, more pleasant than my real one had ever been, and I am happy to do my part in attempting to bring water to this parched area. Between the volunteer labor, the money that Miss Joan is collecting and any of my own money I might need to contribute, I have every confidence that this can be done and we will be able to save those ranches and farms."

That being said, Alan looked at Raegan pointedly. "Do you believe me?"

"You do have a hypnotic way of presenting your point of view," she allowed.

"I guess that you bring out the best in me," he told Raegan warmly.

Raegan laughed, shaking her head. "And if I believe that, then there was the one about the three bears," she answered.

"When did you become so cynical?" he asked, a smile playing on his lips.

That was easy enough to answer, she thought. "From the very first day that you walked into my life."

He leaned in toward Raegan, his eyes holding her captive. "You don't really mean that," he told her.

"Well, I would have at one point," she admitted. "But I guess that you're right," she conceded. "Still, you have to realize that after all those summers that you spent in Forever, driving me crazy, it is kind of difficult to forget about the way you used to behave and just take you at face value now."

"I will be the first one to admit that I wasn't exactly a sterling person when I was younger, and for that, I truly apologize," he told Raegan.

"I guess it would be considered bad form at this point to hold your past behavior against you," she allowed. She put her hand out to him. "Truce," she announced.

"Truce," he agreed, shaking the hand she offered. "You've already done a great deal to make me feel that you've decided to forget about my past behavior and just move forward," Alan told her.

She accepted his words in good faith. "I suppose that bearing a grudge isn't going to get us anywhere, is it?" she asked.

"No," Alan agreed. "It's not."

Alan glanced around, aware that although they had been sitting among a number of other people who had attended the getting-acquainted party, at this point, most of those people had gone inside, drawn by the music.

That same overwhelming feeling washed over him. The one that had him wondering what her lips tasted like and if they were as sweet as they looked.

The next moment, Alan gave in to his curiosity.

Leaning in closer, he managed to create all sorts of shock waves shooting through her. And then, as her breath caught in her throat, his lips touched hers.

Raegan didn't pull away.

Chapter Fourteen

And just like that, Raegan's entire world turned upside down. She could feel her heart accelerating, her pulse pounding at a rate she had never even remotely experienced before.

Raegan knew she should pull back, rise to her feet and immediately create a space between them.

A *wide* space.

But the plain truth of it was, she didn't want to. What she wanted was to have this wild, exhilarating feeling continue forever. She wanted to melt into the sensation he had suddenly caused to spring up inside of her.

Raegan tried not to moan as she absorbed his caress, drawing it into her.

What had started out as little more than idle curiosity on Alan's part suddenly mushroomed into an exceptional, wondrous sensation that captivated him and all but held him a virtual prisoner.

Who would have ever thought Raegan was capable of creating these explosive, wonderful feelings that were undulating through him. Rather than move back and terminate the contact, Alan continued it, cherishing it and glorying in it.

But after a prolonged moment, Alan knew that he couldn't allow himself to continue with this indulgence. If anyone should come out of the saloon and see him kissing Raegan—or think that they were observing her kissing him—the result would be the same: Raegan would wind up being embarrassed.

He couldn't allow that to happen.

For her sake.

Drawing his lips away, Alan saw the look of surprise on her face. His explanation was immediate.

"They might be looking for us," he told her. "Maybe we should go inside."

Raegan could hardly believe that Alan would

wind up being the sensible one here, not her. But she was not about to argue with what he was saying. The one-time bane of her existence was making sense.

A lot more sense than she could make right now.

"Of course we should," she agreed, rising to her feet.

She was about to pick up her empty paper plate, but Alan moved her hands away, taking her plate and placing it on top of his own.

"I can throw this away for you," he told Raegan.

Being independent almost to a fault, she was about to tell him he didn't need to bother, but she had a feeling that might not come across the right way. After all, if she was being honest about it, Alan was just attempting to be nice. It just wasn't something she was accustomed to. She knew she needed to keep that foremost in her mind and stop blocking him at every turn.

Nodding her head, she withdrew her hands and told him, "Be my guest."

The smile Alan flashed at her went straight to her gut. As did the way his eyes slowly washed over her.

"I'd love to," he told her just before he led the way back inside.

The rest of the party went by really quickly, dissolving in a swirl of voices and people interacting with one another.

Every so often, she would see Alan looking at her, and a host of thoughts would suddenly spring up inside her head. They were thoughts she was determined to block, even if it wasn't easy.

By the time Raegan finally left Murphy's with her family and got home, she was totally exhausted. But that exhaustion didn't allow her to actually sleep.

She tossed and turned like a spinning top, desperately looking for just a few minutes of rest.

For the most part, sleep eluded her.

When her grandfather got up early the following morning, he found Raegan not only up, but also already working in the barn.

Mike Robertson stood back and watched his granddaughter in silence for a moment, then finally asked, "Shouldn't you be getting ready to meet up with Alan and the others? After all, according to what he'd said yesterday, this is supposed to be the project's first day. Or has that been changed for some reason?"

Preoccupied, she hadn't even heard her grandfather come up behind her. It took all she had not to jump or cry out in surprise.

Regaining control over herself, she answered in a completely calm voice, "No, it hasn't been changed."

Despite the control she exercised, her grandfather sensed that something was off. "You seem kind of tense, Rae," he noted. "Is there something wrong?"

Her first instinct was to just say she was experiencing first-day jitters. But it had always been her grandfather's first rule of behavior that no lies should ever be exchanged.

Mindful of that, Raegan took a deep breath and said, "He kissed me."

Mike didn't have to ask his granddaughter who the "he" was in this case. Instead, he smiled at Raegan. "Well, it's about time."

Stunned, she looked at her grandfather in surprise. Had he been expecting this to happen? "What?"

Mike didn't bother to repeat himself. Instead, he asked, "Did you like it?"

Raegan didn't see any reason to pretend to be

surprised by her grandfather's question. Instead, she sighed, and mumbled, "Yes."

Mike smiled as he nodded. "That's all that counts," he told her.

That caught her off guard and she stared at him. "How did you know?"

Her grandfather laughed. "Honey, *everybody* knew. Except maybe for the two of you." He continued, "There was enough electricity flashing between the two of you to keep Benjamin Franklin's kite lit up for years. Anything else?" he asked her, curious.

Raegan shrugged, still rather surprised by her grandfather's take on this. "No."

"Fine, then come on into the house and have some breakfast," he urged, turning to lead the way back in. "If this turns out to be a full day, the way I suspect it will, there's no telling when you'll be back or get another chance to eat."

"Yes, Grandpa," Raegan responded dutifully as she walked alongside him.

Mike chuckled, then slipped his arm around her shoulders. "That's my girl. And just remember," he told her, "don't feel like you have to work harder than anyone else. You don't have anything to prove to anyone…least of all to yourself," her grandfather stressed.

* * *

Alan stood watching as various people he had broken bread with just yesterday slowly began to fill the field where, it had been decided, the initial work would begin.

Standing there amid the engineers he had brought with him to Forever, Alan still had to express his overall surprise.

"This is a really a great turnout," Chris Collins commented as he saw even more ranchers and farmers join their ranks.

"If they all wind up digging those ditches and laying the pipes into the ditches, the work might ultimately be done ahead of schedule," Greg asserted. "And, if it does, that'll really be a first," he told the others.

"They are a really hard-working bunch of people," Raegan attested, walking up behind the engineers. "They like pulling their own weight whenever they can."

Alan turned around, pleased to see her there. He had to admit that he'd had his doubts after he had foolishly given in to temptation and kissed her.

"You're here," he declared.

"Why wouldn't I be? I'm part of the town," Raegan reminded him.

"Yeah, but you're a female and this is going to be hard, physical work," Logan protested.

Alan didn't even pretend to hide his amusement. "I wouldn't go there if I were you, Logan," he told his friend. "Raegan works with the horses on her grandfather's ranch. Part of that includes breaking them in and seeing to those horses' needs whenever necessary. She's definitely not afraid of working hard," he added, a touch of pride slipping in.

Raegan hadn't shared any of this with Alan. It would have sounded much too much like bragging. "How would you know that?" she asked.

"Riley told me. At least, I think it was Riley. Could have been Roe," Alan amended. "The only thing I know for sure was that it wasn't you."

"Because of the dimple," she ventured.

"Among other things," he answered with a wide smile.

At that point, there was a large group gathered around them. Chris tapped Alan on the shoulder, calling his attention to the business at hand.

"Looks like everyone who plans to be here *is* here," he told Alan. "I think it's time to get started."

And so it was, Alan thought. He waited until

the men—and a few of the women who had come along—quieted down. Then he proceeded to outline the immediate task at hand, and divided up various duties among the people who had arrived. He had some of them digging ditches along with Logan and him. The rest, including Chris and Greg, he put to work laying the trenches that would eventually hold the pipes, which would divert water into the reservoir that was going to be constructed.

Raegan quietly listened as Alan gave his pep talk to the people gathered around him. It was short and to the point. At the very beginning, and then again at the end, he expressed his thanks to all of them for having turned out to work next to one another—and him.

When he finished, Alan looked at Raegan. "And, if at any time," he said in the same sort of voice he had used to address the crowd, "you feel a need to stop, by all means stop."

She was about to tell him not to hold his breath, but she decided that he actually meant well, so all she told him was "Thanks. Now let's get started."

Her remark was like hearing a starter pistol going off and it was met with a cheer. At that point, everyone who had shown up divided into two groups and got to work.

Work continued for hours.

The locals who were pitching in stopped only long enough to partake of the lunches that Miss Joan sent over to celebrate their first full day of work.

Alan was the last one to finally stop digging and take a break. Sitting down cross-legged beside Raegan in the shade of a towering pine tree, he took a long drink from the bottle of water that had been included in the bagged lunch.

"You know, the way I remembered Miss Joan from my childhood is that she was this thin, older, unsmiling woman who, when I first met her, I thought might actually be a wicked witch. Just when did she turn into this fairy-godmother type?" he asked Raegan.

"That was always her secret identity," Raegan told him with a laugh. "I think this grumpy-old-lady act was her way of keeping some people at arm's length while she saw just what those people she hadn't formed an opinion about were made of. If she thought you were a worthwhile person, she would have your back entirely, although, again, at her own pace."

The explanation tickled Alan as he shook his

head. "And here I thought that people who lived out here were just simple folk without a complicated thought in their heads. Boy, was I ever wrong," he commented.

"Well, it looks like you just realized your error," she told him. "Just shows that even you have a lot of room for growth." After taking a long sip from her own bottle of water, she let out a deep, contented sigh, then put the remnants and wrapper back into the paper bag that it had arrived in. Dusting off her hands, Raegan rose to her feet.

"Calling it a day?" Alan asked.

"No," she replied. "Why would you say that? It's only midday," she pointed out. "I'm going back to work."

"You know you can take a longer break," Alan told her.

"I know," she replied. "But I think I should get back to work while I still have some energy left to *do* the work," Raegan told him. "Something tells me that my arms are *really* going to ache tomorrow morning, and I'm not sure just how much digging I'll be up to doing."

"If that happens," he told her, "you can take the day off tomorrow. This is all volunteer work," he reminded Raegan. The next moment, he raised his voice, addressing the group that had taken a break with him and Raegan, and were scattered around them. "That goes for the rest of you. If you find yourselves hurting too much after today, please don't hesitate to take the day off. As long as you can show up in a day or two—or three—that'll be good enough for me. For us," he amended, nodding at Logan and Greg. "We're not looking to work you to death," he said, referring to the other engineers working alongside of him when he said "we're."

With that, he rose to his feet beside Raegan. "Okay," he said to her amicably, "let's get back to it."

Alan, his engineer friends and all of the townspeople who had come out to volunteer their services continued to work until the sun went down.

Finally, he decided that enough was enough.

"Okay, everyone, I think we can call it a day. Every one of you did an excellent job today. I honestly feel as if we got a lot done, considering that this was just the first day we've been working together, and for some of you, this is totally foreign work."

"Most of us are used to working with our hands

one way or another and none of us are afraid of doing any kind of manual work," one of the ranchers, who had been one of the first to show up this morning, told Alan.

"Well, we appreciate it and we look forward to seeing as many of you as can make it tomorrow," Alan said as he sent the volunteers home.

"Does that go for me, too?" Raegan asked after she had waited for the major group of volunteers to leave.

"Absolutely," Alan told her. "As long as your grandfather doesn't need you on the ranch."

"My grandfather had three hired hands working for him before my sisters and I even started going to school," Raegan told him. "Grandpa will be okay. Besides, he was the one who said that at least one of us from the family should be working on this project with you." She saw Alan's bemused look and decided to explain further. "Let me put it this way—it was a choice of either him or me, and my grandfather's back does give him trouble every now and then, so I was not about to let him do any digging."

Raegan began to walk away, then abruptly stopped. "By the way, what's on tap for tomorrow?" she asked.

"More of the same," he told her.

She nodded. "I look forward to it," she told him.

Alan looked at her for a long moment, "Yeah," he told her in all seriousness. "Me, too."

Chapter Fifteen

The aches and pains were finally beginning to dissipate.

As Raegan had predicted, the day after her first full day of digging, she could have sworn that every single bone in her body ached something fierce.

Even as she attempted exercising mind over matter and tried to deny that she was in any sort of pain by moving as if her arms, shoulders and back were *not* in utter agony, the pain definitely registered and came through with every single move she made.

But, by day number four, the pain she had initially experienced had begun to fade to the point that it was totally manageable. She was able to work right beside Alan and dig the trenches she knew were so necessary.

Raegan wasn't working very long when she took note of the deep frown that was on his face. She drew her own conclusion as to why it was there.

"You know, if I'm getting in your way, you can just point me in another direction and I can go dig there," Raegan offered. From the first day, she noticed that everyone was working in pairs, but as far as she could see, that wasn't altogether necessary, especially if Alan had decided he didn't want to work with her.

Alan had only started digging today a short while ago. His goal was extending the ditch and its accompanying pipeline that he and Raegan had begun laying down yesterday morning.

"You're not getting in my way," he protested. "I'm just worried that this is going to wind up being too much for you," he told her honestly. "After all, digging like this is really hard work and I don't want you to feel as if you're being pressured to—"

"Don't worry," Raegan responded. "I don't

feel pressured. If anything, you're creating an obstacle course for me. I'm fine," she assured him, then said with feeling, "Really."

Alan looked far from convinced. Memories of their competition came back to him.

"You wouldn't tell me even if you weren't fine," he said. "Am I right?"

"Possibly," she acknowledged with a vague wave of her hand. "But for now, as long as I can do the work, let me do it. Deal?" she asked.

"Well, I don't really have a choice, do I?" Alan answered. "But, I just want you to remember, if anything happens to you, your grandfather is going to kill me."

An infectious grin played on her lips. "I guess that everything has a silver lining, doesn't it?" Raegan said. And then she told him more seriously, "Don't worry, my grandfather won't blame you. He knows how really stubborn I can be once I set my mind to something."

"Well, that's not exactly a secret," Alan pointed out.

"Then what are you worried about?" she asked him. "Bottom line, no one's going to be blaming you."

That really wasn't the point, Alan thought. He

was just trying to look out for her. "Maybe I'm not worried about anyone blaming me."

He had lost her. Just what was he getting at? "Then what are you worried about?" she asked.

Did he have to draw her a road map? "You," he finally answered.

The blunt answer threw her. It took her a moment to gather herself together. "I appreciate that," she finally responded. "But right now, with this drought showing no signs of abating or going away, you have bigger things to worry about than my sore muscles. Hand me back my shovel, Alan, and let me get to work."

Alan knew there was no point in arguing with her, especially since he felt that he wasn't going to win. And, if he was being honest about it, he did admire her determination.

He picked up a shovel and handed it to her. "Have I ever told you that you are the most stubborn woman I have *ever* met?" he asked.

Taking the shovel from him, she replied, "No, at least not today."

Raegan glanced over her shoulder. She saw that a number of locals had arrived and were getting down to work. "We're burning daylight, White Eagle," she informed him crisply.

Alan stared at her. He had gotten here at his

usual time, but it didn't change the fact that it was early.

"It's seven in the morning," he pointed out to her.

"Right. Like I said, we're burning daylight," Raegan told him. "You're the boss man, so you can do that, but as for the rest of us, we don't have that luxury."

"You're doing this for free on a volunteer basis," Alan pointed out. "You *provide* that luxury."

But Alan found himself talking to Raegan's back. Shovel in hand, she had jumped into the ditch that she and Alan had spent yesterday and part of the day before digging. Once the pipeline was firmly laid in the trench, they would move on to still another part of the ditch and begin digging there.

"Out of sheer curiosity," Raegan asked Alan several hours later, "how many more of these pipelines are going to have to be laid?"

Alan paused to catch his breath. As was his habit, he demanded twice as much of himself as he did from any of the others, and that included from his engineering friends, Logan, Chris and Greg, as well.

Leaning on his shovel, he gave the question she asked due consideration. When he had mulled it over for a while, he quoted a number for her.

She looked at him, stunned. The number was even higher than she had thought. "You're kidding," she whispered.

"I kid about a lot of things," Alan admitted as he resumed digging, "but this is not one of them."

Taking his words to heart, Raegan started digging again, determined to keep up. Not because she didn't want to give Alan the opportunity to make a flippant comment about her falling down on the job, or falling behind—they had gone beyond that point—but because she wanted to do as much as she possibly could to make decent headway in this self-imposed job she had chosen to do.

Slow and steady was the rule of that day, as well as of every day that followed.

Every day, the locals turned up to work and do that digging with a fair amount of regularity. The faces changed from one day to the next, as well as from one week to the next.

But even though the faces might have changed,

the approximate number of workers, fortunately, remained the same.

"You know," Alan began just before they decided to knock off after yet another day, "I am really impressed with how hard everyone is working, day in, day out. I thought for sure that everyone would start finding excuses to drop out by the time we approached week number three," he marveled. "And more time than that has gone by."

He dusted off his hand against the back of his jeans, then bent down and extended the same hand to Raegan.

"Well," Raegan said, taking the hand he had offered to her and crawling out of the trench she had helped dig, "the people here are mostly hard workers who are an incredibly good bunch of people. And, for the most part, they have a healthy respect for—and fear of—Miss Joan."

She allowed herself a smile as she paused for a moment to catch her breath.

"She's not going to do anything to them... right?" he asked, not exactly a 100 percent certain about his assumption.

"Sometimes the threat of something is even worse than the actual execution of that something," Raegan said, theorizing. "Besides, everyone wants to stay in that woman's good graces," she told Alan.

"Well, I can't argue with that," he admitted. He looked around. His friends appeared to have already called it a day and most of the other workers had either already left, or were getting ready to. "Ready to pack it in for today?" he asked Raegan.

Oh, more than ready, she thought. And then Raegan assessed the scene. "We're almost done with this trench. How many more trenches are there to go?" she asked.

"By my reckoning, I'd say we have less than half a mile of pipe to put down," Alan told her. He didn't want to talk about trenches and pipelines. This was the end of the day and he wanted to empty his mind until tomorrow morning. "Want to get something to eat?" he asked, then added, "My treat."

"Are you asking me out?" she asked, a hint of a smile playing on her lips.

"I guess in a manner of speaking, I am... unless that spooks you," he said, adding a qualifier. "Does it?"

His thoughtfulness surprised her. "I think we're past the point where you spook me and I irritate you," she told Alan.

Her remark threw him for a moment and he looked at her. "I never said that you irritated me."

"You didn't have to," she told him. "I'm pretty good at picking up vibes." That being said, Raegan ran her hand through her hair, doing her best to get it into some semblance of neatness. "All right, let's hit Miss Joan's diner and get some dinner," she told him—and then a thought hit her. "Should we swing by the hotel and pick up your friends?" she asked, thinking that he might want to include them.

"Don't worry about them," he told her. He wanted to have dinner with just her, not with his friends, too. "They're big boys and can definitely provide for themselves." And then he re-thought his words. Maybe there was a reason why she had asked about his friends accompanying them. "Unless you'd feel more comfortable having them around."

"Are you trying to say, in your own 'quaint' way, that I'm afraid of having dinner with you without an armed guard around?" she asked, trying to understand why Alan would say something like that to her.

"I'm just doing my best to second-guess you and cover all the possible bases," he told her nebulously.

"You don't have to bother, White Eagle," she told him, falling back on using his last name, the way she usually did when she was trying her best to make a point. "I wasn't afraid of being around you when I was a kid and I definitely am not now. Now let's go get something to eat before I start gnawing on you," she told him.

He grinned at her. "That might be interesting," he allowed.

"Just get going," she ordered, pointing in the general direction of his truck. "I'll meet you at Miss Joan's diner."

He saluted her like a soldier acknowledging orders.

Alan didn't bother hiding his grin.

They pulled into the parking lot almost simultaneously. Alan was approximately just a beat ahead of her.

Getting out of his truck, he waited until Raégan pulled up one row over.

"Ready to go in?" he asked as she walked up to him.

Raegan nodded, then smiled. "Unless Miss Joan has decided to institute curbside dining," she said.

"I think that's a bit too much to hope for," he

told Raegan. "Besides, right now I'm looking forward to just sitting in a relatively cool spot and *not* perspiring."

"You read my mind," she countered.

If only, he thought with a tinge of wistfulness.

Alan walked up to the diner's front door, then held it open for her. "After you," he told Raegan with a sweeping gesture.

At least half the people he and Raegan had worked with that day were either seated in the diner, or on their way out after grabbing a quick, much-desired bite to eat.

As they made their way to a small table for two, they found themselves directly in Miss Joan's line of vision.

Alan caught himself thinking that the woman was uncanny. No matter where she was in the diner, she always seemed to be able to home in on them.

Just as the thought went through his head, he heard Miss Joan's voice. "Well, look at what the cat just dragged in," she observed, amused, as she carefully looked the pair over. "Didn't think about cleaning up before you came here, did you?"

"The thought of sitting down to one of your outstanding dinners just proved to be far too tempting for us to stop and think things through," Alan told the woman.

Miss Joan looked at him, shaking her head in amusement. "I guess you don't have to be Irish to be able to spout blarney," she told him. "All right, what'll you two have?" she asked as she approached their table.

At this point, Alan wasn't even remotely fussy. He was just hungry. "Whatever you have to offer, Miss Joan."

Miss Joan managed to catch him completely off guard when she replied, "You're not man enough to take what I have to offer."

Surprised, Alan practically choked on the cup of coffee he had just brought up to his lips. Finally managing to clear his throat, he thought he was safe as he asked, "What would you recommend, Miss Joan?"

Without any hesitation, Miss Joan said, "The spitfire sitting next to you, but that's a story for another time."

Raegan didn't hesitate with her reply. "Two with one blow," Raegan marveled. "My hat's really off to you, Miss Joan."

The woman smiled. "That's what I like to hear," she told Raegan. "Now, today's menu is right in front of you, or Alicia can surprise you and bring you the special of the day. The choice is yours," she concluded, looking from Alan to Raegan and then back again.

"I like surprises," Raegan said, pushing aside her menu. Then she looked at Alan and asked, "How about you?"

The corners of his mouth curved. "I'm beginning to," he told her, answering Raegan's question about whether or not he enjoyed surprises.

Deliberately placing his menu down on top of Raegan's, he told Miss Joan, "Make that two surprises."

"Duly noted," the older woman replied. "Alicia," she called out to the server. "Bring these people two specials of the day. We need to keep this young man working hard for Forever's sake."

Alicia looked extremely willing to make Miss Joan's wish her command, and within a few minutes, quickly brought back two specials, setting them down in front of Alan and Raegan.

"Enjoy," Miss Joan instructed with a wave of her hand just before she melted back behind the counter.

Chapter Sixteen

Dinner lasted longer than either one of them had anticipated. Many of the people who were within the diner took advantage of the informal, laid-back setting and stopped by the table where Alan was sitting with Raegan. To a person, they wanted to extend their gratitude to Alan for what he and the other engineers had set up and were currently doing in order to attempt to save Forever's ranches and the handful of farms that existed within the area.

At first Alan attempted to ignore the avalanche of thanks and then he tried to wave it away, but the locals just kept approaching him until, eventually, he just gave up. He sat there and politely listened to the residents talk.

Finally, after watching this go on for a while, Miss Joan made her way into the center of the impromptu gathering.

"If you're really grateful," she told the locals who were surrounding Alan's table, "you'll let the poor man eat in peace. Tomorrow you can all show him how grateful you are by coming back and working as hard as you're capable of doing." Her words effectively hovered over the crowd that was, until now, growing larger and larger around Alan's table.

Alan flashed a smile at Miss Joan as the last of the crowd finally dispersed and went away. "That was very diplomatic, Miss Joan," he commented in a lowered voice.

Miss Joan inclined her head. "I have my moments," she responded. "Now, do you want to take anything to eat with you when you leave?"

"No, thank you. I'm officially stuffed," Alan replied. He looked over toward Raegan. "How about you?"

"If I consume one more morsel," she told him, "I'll explode." Raegan shifted her eyes toward

Miss Joan. "Please tell Angel that she outdid herself," she requested.

"I'll be sure to do that," Miss Joan promised, pleased to be able to give the young woman who had prepared the meal a compliment. In general Miss Joan was stingy when it came to voicing compliments herself, but she was always pleased to be able to pass one on from someone else. "Now, since you're both finished eating, I'd encourage you to leave and go on with your evening."

Alan realized that in her haste to usher them out, the woman had forgotten one very important point. "Wait. I haven't paid for our dinners yet," Alan told Miss Joan, reaching for his wallet.

The look Miss Joan gave him could have stopped a charging rhino in its tracks.

"Yes, you did," she informed him with finality. "Now go before you wind up insulting me."

Raegan leaned in toward Alan and whispered, "I'd do as she says if I were you," just before she slid out from her chair and rose to her feet.

Alan had no choice but to join her. "Thank you very much," he told Miss Joan.

The woman made a short, disparaging noise and, turning on her heel, walked back and got behind the counter.

"I believe that's our cue to leave," Raegan told him, hooking her arm through his and drawing Alan toward the front door.

"I still don't feel right about not paying," he told Raegan once they were out of the diner.

"Trust me, you don't want to insult the woman. Miss Joan paying for dinner is her way of thanking you for what you and the others are doing. I'm sure that if Chris, Logan or Greg stopped by, she'd pick up their tabs, too. Well, maybe not Greg's tab because that might just bankrupt her," Raegan joked, tongue in cheek, "but she would cover at least part of Greg's bill."

Reaching where her vehicle was parked, she turned back toward Alan. "Well, I guess I'll see you tomorrow," she said.

For his part, Alan appeared reluctant to call it a night just yet and said as much. And then he suggested, "Would you like to stop by Murphy's for a nightcap?" When she didn't respond immediately, Alan asked, "Or maybe we can get a drink at the hotel?"

Her eyes met his and she smiled. "I think I'd like that."

"Which one would you like to go to?" he asked, looking for clarification. "Murphy's or the hotel?"

She didn't even have to think about it. "I think the hotel would be quieter. I'm sure that there'll be a lot of people at Murphy's, just like there were at the diner, who would want to express their gratitude that you and your friends came riding to their rescue."

"You make it sound like the guys and I are the cavalry," he commented.

"Well, in a manner of speaking, I guess that you kind of are," she told him.

Things certainly had changed, Alan couldn't help thinking, remembering the verbal exchanges they'd had from a decade ago. Who would have ever thought? he mused.

"Do you want me to lead the way to the hotel, or do you want to lead?" he asked.

Though it wasn't actually necessary, Raegan liked the fact that Alan was giving her a choice of either leading or following him to the hotel. She took it as an indication that he felt they were equals on this playing field, and since he was acting that way, she was more than willing to yield to him.

I'd watch feeling that way if I were you, she warned herself. *That's how mistakes get made.*

Out loud, she told him, "It's your hotel, you can lead the way."

"My pleasure," he said.

The words had just popped out. Alan had no idea why they did and he hoped that she wouldn't suddenly take it the wrong way.

But judging from her expression, he thought a moment later, she wasn't taking the words at anything but their face value.

The trip from Miss Joan's diner to the hotel took only a few minutes. Alan parked his truck in his assigned spot. Getting out, he made eye contact with Raegan and then indicated the first available empty spot in guest parking.

As it turned out, the spot was only a few feet away from his.

Taking her arm, Alan escorted Raegan into the hotel. When they entered the small lobby, he paused as he debated the choice that had presented itself to him.

"What's wrong?" Raegan asked.

"Do you want to go into the hotel bar to get that drink, or go up to my room?" Alan asked, leaving the ultimate choice up to her.

She approached the problem logically rather than going with her emotions. "If we go into the hotel bar to get that drink, you could very well be facing the same problem that you did when we were at Miss Joan's. If your groupies get wind of the fact that you're here, having a drink, they'll gather around and might not want to leave you alone. In all probability, they might want to start buying you drinks."

That wasn't what he'd had in mind, coming here for a drink, Alan thought. He was looking for privacy.

"I'd hardly call them groupies," he said with a dismissive laugh.

"Well, if you did," Raegan told him, "that would just be a sign that your ego was growing at an incredible rate and attaining huge proportions. But if I'm the one saying it, then it can just be construed as a compliment."

Alan shook his head incredulously. "There must be a very winding path inside that head of yours," he observed. "I'll just elect to go with the more flattering description. We'll go to my room," he said, then added, "We can leave the door open if you'd like."

"Why?" Raegan asked innocently, batting her lashes at him. "Are you afraid I'll have my way with you?"

Alan laughed and then shook his head. "I think the word *afraid* is the wrong one to use here. *Hopeful* might be a more apt description for what I'm feeling."

Raegan merely smiled as they got in the elevator. "We'll see," she said vaguely, not about to commit herself.

When the elevator stopped on the third floor, they got off and went down the short hallway. Alan used his key card and they walked into his room.

Raegan looked around as she crossed the threshold. "This is smaller than I expected."

Alan shrugged. "It's got a bed and a desk, which is all I really require," he told her. "Oh, and a shower," he added on as an afterthought. "Can't forget that."

"You really have changed a lot since we were younger," Raegan said, feeling obligated to make that comment. She couldn't imagine the younger Alan saying anything like that.

"How so?" he asked as he walked over to place an order on the hotel phone.

"The Alan I recall liked the outward trimmings of his position in the scheme of things— and they were rather showy."

Alan didn't quite remember it that way, but there could have been an element of truth in her evaluation. Keeping that in mind, he said,

"He grew up," just before he called down to the hotel bar.

Raegan liked the basic honesty of Alan's response. She smiled at him. The smile seemed to burrow directly into his chest. "So I see."

"What would you like?" he asked Raegan, then cleared his throat as he clarified, "To drink."

"Something light. A Singapore sling," she decided. A single drink of that wouldn't cause her to experience any sort of a confusing reaction. It would take more than a single one of those to affect her.

He heard the line on the other end being picked up. Alan identified himself, gave the bartender his room number, then told her the names of the drinks he was ordering. "Send up a Singapore sling and a Black Russian."

The person on the other end promised him that the order would be sent up within the next fifteen minutes, if not sooner.

Thanking the woman, Alan replaced the receiver. "The bartender said that the drinks will be sent up soon," he said to Raegan.

She had begun moving around the room, wondering if her coming up here was such a good idea on her part. There was no doubt in her mind that she was attracted to Alan. That initial attraction had only grown more intense since he had kissed her. But even so, she was afraid that she might have made a mistake, coming up to his room instead of going to Murphy's or grabbing a seat at the hotel bar.

Was she giving him the wrong message? And what, exactly, was the right message?

She no longer knew.

Just then there was a knock on the door. "I guess that business must be slow," Alan commented, going up to the door.

The person on the other side had a tray that was sitting on the table that he was pushing in front of him. The tray had two drinks on it.

"Your drinks, sir," the young man needlessly announced.

"Just set the table over there," Alan instructed. Reaching into his pocket, he took out several bills that he intended to give the young man as a tip. "Thank you."

The man who had brought in their drinks was surprised as he glanced at the bills that had been pressed into his hand.

"No, thank *you*, sir," he said to Alan with feeling.

Raegan caught herself smiling at the young man's unabashed enthusiasm.

Turning toward Raegan after the man left the room, Alan sat down across from her and asked, "What shall we drink to? A successful resolution of the project?"

"There's that," Raegan allowed, picking up her glass. Her eyes held his as she added, "We could also drink to new beginnings."

"New beginnings," Alan repeated. "You mean as in you and me?"

Raegan continued looking at him. Suddenly, she wasn't feeling nearly as confident as she had been a moment ago. Shrugging, she told Alan, "Make of it what you will."

"I will," he told her agreeably, bringing his glass up to his lips. After setting down his own glass, he watched as Raegan took a sip from hers. "Did they get it right?" he asked, nodding at her drink. He knew that the ordinary drinks were easy enough to make, but a drink like a Singapore sling could prove to be a bit tricky.

Focusing exclusively on the drink, she nodded. "Actually, yes, they did."

"Where did you ever learn about a drink like that?" Alan asked.

Raegan looked at him. "Every so often, I get unshackled from the ranch and venture off into the big city."

"I didn't mean that as an insult," he told her. "What I meant was that what you ordered wasn't exactly a commonly known drink."

She was being too sensitive...or maybe too nervous. Trying to backtrack, she said, "I'm adventurous."

"Would you like to have another adventure?" he asked, then realized how that had to have sounded to her. "I meant, would you like me to order another drink for you?"

"I know what you meant," she said, beginning to relax as she gave him a wide, inviting smile. "One drink is fine. I do have to drive home," she reminded him.

"You don't have to drive home right away," he told her. "Actually, I wouldn't advise it."

"What would you advise?" she asked him.

"Well, what I would advise might get me slapped," he admitted.

She felt like her breath had just caught in her throat.

"Why don't you try saying it out loud and see?" she suggested. She had to focus on breathing. Even so, she never took her eyes off him.

Her pulse sped up.

"All right," Alan agreed quietly.

He leaned in and placed his hands ever so

gently on either side of her face. Cupping it softly between his hands, he brought his face down to hers.

He kissed her gently, softly, and as he did, the sensation, the yearning within him, grew steadily more intense, more pronounced, until he finally drew her into his arms and gave in to the emotion that was now too large to contain.

Chapter Seventeen

Initially, when Alan came to Forever to put his plan before the town council, he had had every intention of keeping business and pleasure in totally separate corners.

But somehow, good intentions didn't seem to matter anymore. Not now. Not when Raegan's mouth tasted as sweet as it did. Not when the flames of desire seemed to flare so urgently all through him.

Alan held Raegan against him, caressing her. He wanted her with a tremendous craving that seemed to infiltrate every single pore of his body.

But even though it would have come close to almost killing him, he waited for Raegan to tell him to stop, to back away. And if she did, he would have.

But she didn't.

Raegan didn't say anything.

Instead, she seemed to completely surrender herself to this incredible feeling that had seized her in its grip.

When Alan began to unbutton her blouse, he suddenly forced himself to stop before he couldn't.

Breathing heavily, he pulled back his head, and although he desperately wanted to devour her mouth, he forced himself to make certain everything was okay. He asked, "Are you all right with this?"

It took Raegan a full moment to catch her breath so that she could answer him. And then she simply said, "You'd know if I wasn't."

Awed, Alan looked at her now. It was as if a gun had gone off, releasing the desire that was throbbing so urgently throughout his entire body. He kissed Raegan over and over again, even as his eager fingers undid the row of buttons that ran down along her blouse.

The feel of his fingers gliding gently along

her skin triggered Raegan's reaction. She began to swiftly undo the buttons along Alan's shirt.

Within moments, she was tugging the material off his shoulders and down along his arms.

Without pausing, Alan shrugged out of the remainder of his shirt, casting it aside without even looking at it.

His attention was completely focused on the woman on his lap.

And then, without a word, he rose to his feet, picked her up in his arms and carried her to his bed.

All the while, there was a part of him that was paying very strict attention to make sure that no matter what he was experiencing, his behavior wouldn't cause him to cross a line he had sworn to himself he wouldn't cross. Even in the midst of this swirling desire he was experiencing, he wanted to make sure that what was happening was mutual.

Whatever went on between them, he was determined that it had to be shared. He refused to make it anything else.

Her heart was hammering so hard, Raegan was certain that Alan had to have heard it. She knew without any question that she had.

And still, she wanted more, *needed* more.

This was everything she had ever thought it would be…and so much more.

More clothing was flung off and discarded, both his and hers, tossed aside like unwanted barriers, without so much as a second glance cast in their direction.

And still, the dance continued, his mouth igniting a blaze within her that refused to abate, refused to lessen even so much as a fraction of an inch.

If anything, Raegan could feel her desire flare and increase, like a bonfire that had suddenly been whipped up and was now raging completely out of control.

Raegan could hardly believe that this was the same person she had known all those years ago, the same young boy who had driven her so crazy.

Was *still* driving her crazy, but in a completely different way than he had ever done before.

Their naked bodies touched and tangled, and every time they did, so many more sparks were felt, more desire filled up the spaces that existed, nurturing heat and a heightened passion that rose up to the sort of caliber that Raegan could not ever remember experiencing.

Alan had trouble believing this was the same competitive young woman who had, just this afternoon, worked so hard right alongside him. Raegan seemed totally different to him right at this moment.

Nothing else seemed to matter to him at this moment in time except having her, making endless love with her.

Not his work, not his promise to bring water to these parched ranches and farms. Nothing but having Raegan in the fullest, most complete sense of the word.

A hunger the likes of which he had never known before urged him on to kiss every single inch of her heaving body, to draw his lips along her nude, trembling skin.

Tracing a hot, moist trail over her body, he anointed it and proceeded to make every single inch he came in contact with his own.

Alan heard her moan.

The sound resonated within him, turning him on even more than he had already been turned on.

Lightning in a bottle, that was what she was experiencing, Raegan thought. Lightning that was going to touch base and then explode within her at any second.

Raegan forced herself to block out what was happening in her body. As soon as she could,

Raegan suddenly turned the tables on Alan, and with deft, clever fingers, she worked her magic and managed to arouse him to a level that took him completely by surprise.

He felt as if his ceiling had just been raised up to immeasurable heights.

And just when Raegan believed that she had completely captured him, Alan suddenly reversed their positions again and, keeping her on her back, his eyes holding her prisoner, Alan slowly merged their bodies until they felt as if they had become one.

He heard Raegan sharply drawing in her breath, and for a second, he was worried that making their bodies one had proven to be too much for her.

But then, as Alan began to move within her, Raegan urgently mimicked his movements, matching them stroke for stroke and going increasingly faster with each pass.

Much faster than they had been going just a moment before.

The tempo increased to the point that neither one of them could back away or even contemplate stopping. They could only hold on tightly to one another until the journey came to an explosive, completely satisfying end.

Raegan continued clinging to Alan as, ever so slowly, she descended back to earth, a feeling of well-being mushrooming within her until the wondrous sensation finally abated and faded away.

Breathing hard, Raegan waited until her heart finally stopped pounding and her pulse finally stopped throbbing.

When a sort of calm finally returned, she turned her body directly into his.

"That was a surprise," she whispered when she could trust herself to form words.

The smile curving the corners of his mouth spread until it all but encompassed his entire face.

"That goes both ways," he confessed. Gathering Raegan to him, he drew her closer until they were almost occupying the very same space. "You know, I never thought that you could actually make the world go away."

"Is that a good thing?" Raegan asked, struggling to think clearly. Her body felt as if it was still vibrating.

"Oh, yes, it's a good thing," he assured her, then said with emphasis, "A *very* good thing." He looked at her in absolute wonder. "You know, until just now, I would have never thought that you could have made me even remotely feel the way I felt just now."

"Felt," she repeated. "As in past tense?" she asked.

"Well, yes, I guess so," he answered uncertainly. "In a manner of speaking."

Her eyes were shining when she looked up at him. "How do you feel about going at it for Round Two?"

He felt as if doing that might be pushing things on his part. "Are you sure you're up to it?"

Alan realized his mistake immediately.

"Brace yourself, White Eagle," she warned him. "It's going to be a very bumpy night."

The old line from a classic movie had his smile growing even wider. "Oh, I think I can handle it," he told her, turning into Raegan. He pulled her into his arms and pressed his lips against hers.

If anything, the second time they made love was even more exhilarating than the first. Alan felt as if he had been raised up to heights he had never even come close to attaining before.

And when it was over, he held Raegan to

him with a little more urgency than he had initially done.

Kissing the top of her head, he asked, "How do you feel about spending the night?" He knew that he really wanted her to.

"Do you usually ask that on a 'first date'?" she asked him, doing her best to keep the smile off her face.

"Actually, no," he answered seriously. "I don't 'usually' ask that at all," Alan told her. Feathering his fingers through her hair, then brushing it off her face, he said, "But this time, it's different."

She wanted to ask him why, but that would sound as if she was fishing for a compliment. Besides, she knew she was going to have to turn him down.

"I'm afraid it is going to be different," Raegan informed him, "because I'm going to have to say no."

Her answer really surprised Alan. He hadn't been prepared for that. "Can I ask why?"

"Because I need to go home. Unless you want my grandfather to come knocking on your door, asking you if you know where I am, which will really not cap off the evening very well."

"Not that I don't think he's a great guy," Alan began, "but why would your grandfather come knocking on my door? Does he suspect there's something going on between us?"

"No. *I* didn't even suspect there was something going on between us," she told him. "Not until tonight turned into what it just did. No, my grandpa would just make the rounds, checking with everyone who might have an idea as to where I might be. My going home just makes it a lot simpler in the long run."

Alan glanced at his watch. It *was* getting late, he realized. "He wouldn't ask you where you've been?"

Raegan smiled, knowing that this had to be difficult for him to understand. "He knows I'm a big girl and I can stay out. This is Forever and its people are predominantly safe and law-abiding. The biggest thing I'd have to fear is a snake crossing my path."

"That's not a euphemism, is it?" Alan asked.

"Nope," she answered, then continued, "I just know that Grandpa would feel better knowing I was safe and sound in my bed. He likes things to be orderly."

Alan nodded, throwing off his covers. "All right, let me get dressed and I'll follow you home."

Now who was being overly cautious, she thought. "You don't have to," she protested. "Go back to bed. I can get home on my own."

"I know, but let me have my illusions," Alan told her. "I know you probably think I don't have any manners, but I do and one of those manners involves making sure a lady gets home."

"Far be it from me to rob you of your illusions," she told him.

Sliding out of bed, she bent down and picked up her scattered clothing, then began to get dressed.

When she glanced behind her, Raegan saw that Alan had stopped getting ready. "You're staring."

"I know." Alan smiled at her. "Grant me a moment. I'm staring at the most beautiful vision I've ever come across."

She laughed, shaking her head. "Just what was it that was in that drink you had brought up?"

"It wasn't the drink that got me drunk," he told her. "It was you." He ran his hands along her arms, creating an intense, intimate moment between them. "All those years that I knew you, I realize now that I never knew you at all."

"Very poetic," Raegan acknowledged. She

paused for a moment. "I guess I didn't know you, either." She grinned mischievously. "You're not nearly the annoying, know-it-all I thought you were."

"I'm flattered... I think," Alan answered. "Was that your idea of a compliment?"

She merely grinned wider. "I'll let you figure that one out."

"I think I'll save that until morning, which is coming on us faster than we think. Are you ready?" he asked.

"I'm dressed—and I'm very ready," Raegan said with a wink. "You really don't have to follow me home."

"I'm being a gentleman," he told her, then added, "Don't deny me one of the few simple pleasures I have."

She placed her hand over her chest. "Far be it from me to do that," she told him, then said, "You can follow me home."

He nodded. "That's better. And for your information, I was going to do just that with your permission or without it."

"Then I guess saying yes to you worked out," she said as they left his hotel room.

His eyes washed over her. His smile was immediate. "I guess it did at that," Alan told her.

Raegan shook her head, but for now, she decided to say nothing. Instead, she just wanted to savor the moment and hold it close to her.

Reality, she knew, would settle in soon enough. As for Alan, he knew when he had lucked out.

Chapter Eighteen

Parking her vehicle by the ranch house, Raegan turned to wave goodbye to Alan. Then, at the very last moment, she darted back to Alan's truck and left one final kiss on his lips.

Stirred, he resisted the temptation to draw her back into his arms. Instead, he pointed toward the front of her house.

"It looks like your grandfather has a light burning in the window," he commented.

"That's either Grandpa's doing, or maybe my mother's," she mused. "Funny, Grandpa and Mom seemed to have adjusted to my sisters living in town, but when it comes to me…" Her voice trailed off as she shook her head and then shrugged.

"I'm sure if your sisters still lived at home, your grandfather and mother would be worried about them as well." He looked a tad wistful as he told her, "All I can say is that you're actually lucky to have someone worry about you."

Raegan realized that Alan was referring to the fact that his parents had been more concerned with how his actions reflected on them than if he was happy doing what he was doing, or if he was doing something that actually made him feel proud of himself.

Raegan nodded. "Maybe you're right," she acknowledged. And then she said, "I'll see you at work tomorrow."

"Count on it," he promised.

With that, Alan slowly drove away.

Turning, Raegan made her way up the front steps. As quietly as possible, she let herself into her house, then slowly locked the door behind her.

Despite the hour, she found both her grandfather and her mother in the living room, playing cards. Raegan was surprised, to say the least.

"Isn't it a bit late for you two to be up?" she asked them.

"We could say the same thing to you," Mike said to his granddaughter.

She couldn't read the expression on his face so she decided to just give him the very basics. "After work, some of us went to grab a bite to eat at the diner," she told her grandfather.

Mike glanced at his treasured watch, the one his wife had given him on their very last anniversary together. The expression on his face said that the hour was late.

"Just how slowly did you chew?" he asked Raegan.

She shrugged and smiled. "You taught me not to gulp my food, remember?" Raegan said matter-of-factly. "Well, as you so subtly pointed out, it is late and I need to get up early for work tomorrow, so unless there's anything else, I'm going to go to bed. See you tomorrow," Raegan cheerfully told the pair as she headed toward the stairs and went up.

Mike waited until his granddaughter was upstairs and out of earshot before he looked at his daughter-in-law. "What do you think?" he asked, the rest of his question going unspoken.

Rita smiled. "I think that the long feud between Raegan and Alan is finally over."

Mike nodded his head. "I think you might be right," he agreed. Smiling, he turned the image of his granddaughter over in his head. "She did have that certain kind of glow about her."

Rita nodded. "I think so, too." And then his daughter-in-law looked at the cards that were left on the coffee table. "I think I'm too happy, not to mention too wired, to sleep," she told her father-in-law.

"You want to play another hand?" Mike offered, picking up the cards and beginning to expertly shuffle them.

Rita smiled gratefully at her father-in-law. "Don't mind if I do."

Their growing attraction notwithstanding, Raegan and Alan continued to work diligently, digging irrigation ditches and laying pipelines seven days a week, ever mindful that even drier weather was waiting in the wings to envelop the area.

The main focus for Alan, the other engineers and the people who were working beside him was to lay the pipelines for the remaining irrigation system. Once that was done—and it was getting close to that point—he planned to build and then fill the new reservoir.

No matter how much he tried to block the thought, Alan couldn't help but feel that they were all racing against time. He had to keep in mind that if a wildfire did suddenly break out and scorch the area, which had been known to happen, there would be no way to fight that fire if the water conditions in and around Forever remained in the present state.

If that wildfire ever did come, people would wind up losing their ranches and farms, not to mention that both animals and people would be in dire danger.

No one knew this better than Alan and he made sure that he kept the volunteer laborers working accordingly.

But at no time did he make any demands on those laborers that he didn't first make on himself.

More than once, as time marched on, Alan tried to encourage Raegan to either take the day off, or to at least work a little slower.

She told him, in no uncertain terms, how she felt about that advice. "When you kick back, White Eagle, I'll kick back. Meanwhile, you need to stop telling me what to do."

Alan merely shook his head. "You never did take direction very well."

Raegan's mouth curved. "At least there's nothing wrong with your memory or your hearing."

The smile he flashed her went straight into her gut like a swift arrow.

"Maybe it could do with a little bit of a reminder," he told her. "Are you up for dinner in my hotel room tonight?"

She didn't even have to think about it. "I could be persuaded."

"Good. Consider yourself persuaded," he said, getting back to work.

But as he did, Alan noticed that Raegan *wasn't* working just yet. "Something wrong?"

"Well, I am going to need a *little* more persuading than that," Raegan told him loftily.

He looked at her in all seriousness. "All right, you name it, I'll do it."

She had intended that in a teasing manner and hadn't expected Alan to take it so seriously. For the most part, even though he wasn't a very private person, he wasn't exactly very vocal about his feelings, either.

This was, Raegan thought, a whole new side to him.

"I'll get back to you on that," she finally responded.

"I'll hold you to that," Alan told her. "As a matter of fact, I'll hold *you*."

Raegan could feel the heat rising within her. She was very aware of her surroundings. "People are staring," she told him between lips that were barely moving.

Her response tickled him. "I don't mind if you don't."

"Later" was all she told him.

Turning away, though, Raegan couldn't erase the wide grin from her face.

It continued that way between them for a while in the coming days. They would work almost nonstop during the day, and then, when the last tool had been put away for the evening, Alan and Raegan would adjourn to his hotel room and enjoy one another's company.

Alan found that this contact completely revitalized him. Rather than grow tired of these moments of passion, or feel as if the passion was growing old, it gave him something to look forward to, a way to be instantly reinvigorated.

"You work too hard," Raegan told Alan one

evening after they had enjoyed one another in his hotel bed.

Smiling down at the woman in his arms, Alan slowly pushed aside the hair from her face. "I don't consider making love with you as working," he told her innocently.

Raegan pretended to swat his hand away. "I wasn't talking about you making love with me. I was referring to the actual work you do. You know that you're pushing yourself much too hard," she chided.

Alan shrugged away her concern. "The work needs to be done and the faster it is, the better. I check the weather report first thing every morning. I feel like there's this big clock hanging over my head and the minutes are ticking away superfast."

Raegan shook her head. "You're being too hard on yourself, Alan," she told him softly. "The work that's been done so far is a great deal more than anyone would have expected at this point."

Since she saw she wasn't getting through to him, Raegan continued, "Miss Joan is very pleased with what you've accomplished, and trust me, the woman practically has a death grip on words of praise. She does not dispense them easily."

"Well, if you feel that way about what we've accomplished, maybe you can stay the night," he suggested. Alan saw the doubt creep into her expression. While he was not about to push his point, he did want to make his case. "Your grandfather and mother have to suspect something by now. You've been coming over to my hotel room practically every night."

"I'm just not ready to talk about it with them," she told Alan. "And you know that would be the next step once our 'arrangement' is out in the open."

Alan gazed at her and, in all seriousness, he asked, "Raegan, are you ashamed of sleeping with me?"

"Oh, no," she quickly denied with feeling. "I just want to hold on to this so-called 'secret' for a little while longer." Raegan smiled ruefully. "You probably think I'm silly."

"Not silly," he contradicted, then supplied the word that did come to mind for him. "Sweet. I think you're being very sweet," he told her, pressing a kiss to her forehead. Then, with a soul-felt sigh, he gave in. "Okay, get dressed. I'll follow you home."

She had given up trying to argue him out of doing that. "In a minute," she murmured, brushing her lips against his.

They didn't leave his hotel room for almost another hour.

The reservoir was finally making some headway and beginning to look like what it was intended to be. Building it from the ground up was slow going, even with Logan in charge. But little by little, the reservoir was taking shape and getting done.

The design wasn't for a large reservoir. The purpose was for it to hold and bring in enough water to supply the much-needed irrigation to the increasingly parched ranches and farms in the area.

When Alan had begun this project, he had despaired that it might never get done, certainly not in time. But now it was beginning to look as if there was an actual end in sight.

Word had it that Miss Joan was so hopeful about the project, she and her husband, Harry, were actually planning to come and review the work that had been done and to see just how much more there was still left to do.

And, being Miss Joan, when she finally did

come to see how things were progressing, she brought baskets filled with food and drink. Because she knew she needed help, Miss Joan made sure to have her husband and his grandson there to help distribute the food.

The moment the workers saw her driving up in her vehicle, word quickly spread around the encampment. Everyone stopped working, gathering together as they all looked at the woman and her family hopefully.

"Don't stop working on our account," Miss Joan told Alan and the people he had laboring beside him.

Even so, Alan temporarily retired the pickax he had been swinging. "We needed the break, anyway," he told Miss Joan with a smile. "No matter which way you approach it, this is really backbreaking work."

"Well, if you're going to stop working," she told Alan philosophically, "you might as well eat to fuel that waning energy of yours."

Climbing out of her vehicle, she turned toward her husband and his grandson. "Harry, Chase, a little help here."

It wasn't so much of a request as it was an order on her part. The two men knew exactly what she was requiring of them.

Harry and Chase removed a number of very large baskets, each holding sandwiches, fruit and other food to distribute among the laborers.

While the male members of her family went about distributing the food, Miss Joan watched the activity taking place happily. "Just my small way to let you all know how greatly appreciated your efforts are. This whole thing would be taking a lot longer if it weren't for all of you. As a matter of fact, we'd all be up that creek without any water to paddle through or navigate in if it weren't for your efforts and your ingenuity," she said.

Miss Joan's sharp hazel eyes took all the workers in one by one. "Thank you," she declared. Then, looking at her husband and his grandson, she announced, "All right, boys, let's go. The diner's not going to run itself and we've been gone too long."

About to get into her vehicle, Miss Joan paused for a moment to look at Alan and then Raegan. "He's a good man," she pronounced with a nod of her head.

And then, with that, she got into her vehicle and closed the door behind her. The next moment, Chase was driving the couple back to the diner.

Raegan looked at Alan, wondering if he had gotten the same impression that she had. "Am I crazy," she asked in a lowered voice, "or did Miss Joan just give us her blessings?"

"You got that impression, too, huh?" Alan asked her, then smiled. "The woman never fails to surprise, does she?"

Raegan laughed softly. "Just when you think you know what to expect, she pulls the rug out from under you," Raegan marveled, then asked, "You ready to get back to work?"

"I thought you'd never ask," he responded with a wide smile.

And with that, Alan got back to work right beside Raegan.

Chapter Nineteen

Although Alan had worked on building a reservoir before and felt that he knew what to anticipate, building this particular reservoir proved to be more involved and thus took longer than Alan had foreseen.

Even though the actual reservoir was not a large one by comparison to other reservoirs that existed in some of the larger cities, it still had to be constructed to accommodate the plans that had been drawn up for this particular area in Texas.

In order to build the reservoir, a great deal of equipment had to be rented.

Very quickly, this was no longer just a simple project. Alan and the others, both the group of volunteer laborers and the professionals that he had to hire and bring in, were busy from morning to night.

He was rather amazed that Raegan never lost a step working alongside of him, although he had to admit that he did push himself harder. But then, because of the nature of his job, he had to be everywhere.

"I hurt in places I didn't even know I had," Alan confessed one evening to Raegan as he was lying on his hotel bed. Although he had initially attempted to talk her out of it, he finally allowed Raegan to apply some salve to his shoulders and back.

With careful, hard, even strokes she massaged the salve in.

"Just relax," Raegan told him, diligently attempting to work out the kinks.

Alan sighed. For the first time that day, the aches and pains that had been throbbing throughout his body had finally begun to recede…a little.

"Where did you learn how to do this?" he asked.

"Just something that came naturally to me, I guess," she told him.

Alan turned around until he was flat on his back. He took her hands in his, looking them over carefully.

"You're an unexpected treasure. I'm tempted to never let you go."

Raegan looked at him, amused at his choice of words. Words she had her doubts that he really meant. "Is that a promise, or a threat?"

The smile that came to Alan's lips worked its way into his eyes.

"You decide," he told her.

Raegan's eyes met his. "I promise I'll let you know when I do."

Taking her hands in his again, Alan pressed a warm kiss to them.

"Stay the night," he coaxed her. He had been making that request every evening now since the first time they had made love.

Her answer was always the same. This time was no different.

"Soon," she promised.

Soon, he was beginning to think, was never going to come, but Alan refused to press the issue any more now than he had initially. Whatever was going to happen—or not happen—ultimately between them was entirely up to Raegan, he thought.

Finally, although it felt like forever, the big moment came. The irrigation ditches that brought in water from the Rio Grande were finally connected to the reservoir.

The whole town turned out to watch as water slowly flowed into the reservoir and filled it. It was a silent promise that if the drought did continue and a wildfire broke out, there would be enough water available to put out that fire.

The relief that rippled throughout the crowd was felt by everyone.

Forever was as safe as it could be, given the circumstances.

Just as when the project had initially begun, Miss Joan called for a party. Thanks to the combined efforts of Miss Joan and the Murphy brothers, there was no shortage of food or drink...or music. The celebration began at noon and lasted way into the wee hours of the night.

But before it wound down, Miss Joan cornered both Raegan and Alan. Putting a thin arm around each of their shoulders, she hugged the couple to her, even though they were both taller than she was.

"I want you to know that the town will always appreciate everything you've done here for us," Miss Joan said.

"I didn't do anything," Raegan protested. "It was all Alan and his engineering friends who spearheaded this operation."

Miss Joan looked at her knowingly. "So you say, Raegan. So you say." It was obvious that the woman thought there was more going on than was just admitted to.

As always, all good things had to come to an end, and slowly, the celebration eventually broke up.

Alan and Raegan were among the very last to leave.

"So what's next?" Raegan asked Alan, even though she really wasn't up to hearing the answer. If she had a vote, she would have wanted this evening to go on forever, despite the fact that it wasn't possible.

"Sleeping for a week," Alan answered as they made their way outside the diner. "Maybe even longer."

She nodded, resigned. She felt incredibly sad, even though, at the outset of all this, she hadn't expected to feel this way. Somewhere along the line, she had fallen in love with this annoying person from her past.

"And after that?" Raegan asked.

"Waking up," Alan answered, a whimsical smile playing on his lips.

"Very funny," she told him. "I meant project-wise."

"I honestly haven't thought that far ahead," he admitted as they walked to the hotel. "What we were doing here was beginning to feel like a never-ending project. Why?" he asked, curious. He turned toward her just as they reached the hotel entrance. "Are you that eager to get rid of me?"

"Get rid of you?" Raegan echoed incredulously. A second later she answered with emphasis. "No! I was just trying to figure out if there was anything in town that could keep you here a while longer," she told him, doing her best to ignore how very heavy her heart felt in her chest.

Alan cupped her cheek for a moment, looking deeply into her eyes. "You," he whispered. And then the next moment, he said, "We can talk about that later. *Much* later. Right now, all I can think about is getting you into bed."

They walked into the hotel and headed toward

the elevator. The lobby they passed through was empty except for one clerk.

"How much time do I have?" Alan asked as they got on the elevator.

She wasn't sure what he was referring to. "How much time do you have for what?"

"Until you turn into a pumpkin and have to go home," he answered. He was surprised that had slipped her mind, considering how she had religiously followed that edict every single evening since their first night together.

"I'm not going home tonight," she told him as they got off the elevator.

"You're not…" His voice trailed off. Alan remembered that Raegan had said she didn't want to get into a discussion with her grandfather and mother about why she wasn't coming home, so she always made sure that she did. "Why?" he pressed, curious. "Did something happen?"

"Just shut up and open your door," she told him, pointing toward his room.

Alan laughed. "Well, since you asked so nicely," he said, slipping his key card into the lock.

The moment the door was opened, Raegan surprised him by throwing herself into his arms. Before he could ask her if anything was wrong, she had sealed her lips to his, silencing any question he was about to ask.

She was completely focused on conveying the extent of her feelings.

His inclination to ask anything at all vanished immediately, as Alan gave in to the heated feelings that were all but drumming, ever so urgently, throughout his entire body.

When they finally did make love sometime later, it was as mind-blowing as it had been that first time...except that it was orders of magnitude better.

Ever so much better.

But beneath it all, Alan could have sworn he detected an extreme urgency in her every move. He wanted to ask her what was wrong, what was driving her like this, but he knew that Raegan would tell him what was going on when she was good and ready to.

They made love not once, but twice.

And then, when their collective energy had completely dissipated, leaving them exhausted, Alan lay there beside her, holding Raegan in his arms, enjoying the way her heart was beating against his.

Gathering her courage, Raegan finally asked, "Are you going to stick around for a while? You know, to make sure that everything is all right?" she added, acutely aware of how hard her heart was pounding.

"Are you suggesting that it's not?" Alan asked her innocently.

"No, but things do go wrong on occasion," she pointed out. "Even things that you were in charge of."

"Then you know about my plan to go slinking off into the night?" Alan asked her with a straight face.

Raegan didn't laugh at his flippant comment. "I'm being serious, Alan," she informed him.

"Well, 'Serious,'" he said, addressing her, "I don't have any plans to leave just yet. The guys and I aren't novices at this, but we do want to make sure that everything is going according to plan. That all the *i*'s are dotted and all the *t*'s are crossed.

"And you're right—sometimes the unforeseen does happen even though we did take every single precaution we could. That's why I'm going to be hanging around for a while. Does that answer your question?"

"Yes," she answered solemnly, turning onto her back. She stared at the ceiling.

"Well, then let me see you smile," Alan told her.

Although her heart wasn't in it, Raegan did her best to comply. "How's that?"

He shook his head. "That looks too much like a grimace. C'mon, Raegan, you can do better than that," Alan urged. And then, before she could attempt to comply with his instruction, he began to weave a series of kisses along her face, then her neck and then both of her shoulders, until he managed to ignite both of them all over again.

The kiss she pressed against his lips was pure fire.

Raegan wove her arms around his neck, then raised and pressed her body up against him.

Mischief danced in her eyes. "How's that?" she asked.

"Better," he told her with a grin. "You're getting warmer…and so am I."

It was in the back of Raegan's mind that her time was limited. Whether Alan left tomorrow or in a week, all of this exquisite behavior was on its way out and she needed to enjoy every single second she had left.

Alan detected the change in her, the desperation, immediately. "Oh, baby," he cried, "what is it?"

But she didn't answer him. Instead, she made

love with him a third and then a fourth time that evening, as if she desperately needed to drain both of them until there was absolutely nothing left to give.

She continued making love with Alan until they were both exhausted. At that point, although they had no memory of it, they fell asleep in each other's arms.

Daylight came like an uninvited intruder, slowly rousing them.

When Raegan opened her eyes, she found Alan looking down at her, his head propped up on his fisted hand.

The first thing she thought of was that there had to be something wrong. She bolted upright, her mind immediately going to the reservoir. Was it that?

"What is it? What's wrong?" Raegan cried.

"There's nothing wrong, Raegan," Alan assured her. "I was just enjoying watching you sleep."

She didn't believe him. "You never did that before."

He didn't argue the point. Instead, he merely said, "You've never stayed the night before."

She had forgotten about that, Raegan thought,

blowing out a breath. Forcing herself to relax, she laid back down on the bed, or tried to. She was far too tense.

"I should be getting back," she told him.

Alan made no effort to get up just yet. "What are you going to tell them?" he asked. He didn't have to say whom he was referring to by "them." He knew that she knew.

"That Miss Joan threw a party for all the workers and we both had a little too much to drink. We came back to your hotel room to sober up. But when we lay down, we both wound up falling asleep."

Alan eyed her doubtfully. "You think they'll believe that? That sounds a little bit flimsy."

She sighed, shrugging her shoulders. "I know, but it's all I've got. I don't generally lie, so I'm not all that good at it. Besides, as I pointed out, I'm a big girl and my grandfather and mother both know it."

"Knowing it and going along with it are two very different things," Alan told her.

Raegan frowned. She hated it when he was right. "All right. What's your suggestion?"

He shook his head. "Nothing at all," Alan answered. "Just pretend there was nothing unusual about you not coming home last night. Let them draw their own conclusions. After all, you *are* an adult and that entitles you to live your life the way you see fit. I'll follow you home, as if nothing has changed."

She had to admit that sounded fairly reasonable to her. "Okay," she told him, tossing aside the sheet that was covering her. "You're on."

He smiled at her warmly, drawing her into his arms. "In a minute," he promised.

But it turned out to be more than a minute. A great deal more.

Chapter Twenty

A week later, Alan stood watching as his friends packed up their things and got ready to leave. There was no doubt about the fact that he was happy for them being able to get back to their lives.

But, admittedly, he felt a little sad for himself.

He was really going to miss those guys, Alan thought. Working together like this had certainly recemented their relationships.

"You know," Alan said to the others, "it's hard to believe that three months could go by so fast."

The expression on Chris's face said he didn't

exactly concur. "Looking back, it felt as if the time just trickled by," he told Alan.

"Well, I sure as hell am going to miss the food…and you guys, too," Greg added as an afterthought.

Logan laughed. "You ask me, I think you're walking away from Miss Joan's diner just in time." Logan reached out and patted Greg's middle. "You look like you're about to split your pants."

Greg sniffed. "Nobody asked you," he pointed out with a touch of indignation.

Alan took in all this banter and grinned. "I am really going to miss this."

"Well, come up with another project and send out a call. We can come back," Chris assured Alan, then looked back at the others. "Right, guys?"

"Right," Greg agreed.

"Count on it," Logan answered.

"I'll definitely be on the lookout for another project," Alan promised. "This dry weather is spreading out through the West."

Alan had wound up paying his friends a relatively modest amount out of his own pocket.

They demurred at first, then decided to take it. It made their working together more acceptable.

One by one, he shook his friends' hands. "It was great working with all of you again," he told them in all sincerity.

"Yeah, yeah," Greg answered. He'd never been much for compliments. "Right back at you."

"It's time that we hit the road, guys," Logan told them.

Alan went down to the front desk with his friends.

The clerk looked surprised when he saw the suitcases. "Are you gentlemen leaving us?" he asked the engineers.

"They are," Alan told the clerk as they left. "I'm not. But don't worry. Now that the job is done, I'll be a paying customer."

The man looked a little uncertain. "Are you sure?" he asked. "There is no rush."

"In a way there is," Alan contradicted. "My integrity demands it."

"Have it your way, sir," the clerk told him. "The first rule of thumb is that the customer is always right, and now that you're a customer…" The clerk flashed a wide, indulgent smile.

Alan nodded. He knew what the man was saying. "Message received."

"Um, Mr. White Eagle?" the clerk began, sounding somewhat nervous again.

To his knowledge, he hadn't left anything unsaid. Alan looked at the clerk quizzically. "Yes?"

The clerk nodded behind Alan. "I believe that one of the Miss Robertsons is waiting to speak to you," he said, indicating Raegan. And then he confided in a lowered voice, "I'm not sure which one."

"That's all right," Alan told him. He turned around to see who the clerk had indicated. And then he smiled as he recognized Raegan. "I am." Moving closer to her, he told her, "You just missed seeing Logan, Chris and Greg leave."

"No, I didn't," she informed Alan. "I said goodbye to each of them and told them that I would miss working with them. They told me that they intended to be back. Do you have anything on tap?" she asked, trying very hard not to sound eager and hopeful.

"No, not yet." A sexy smile worked its way to his lips as he looked at her. And then he slipped his arm through hers, leading her out of the hotel. "Should I be jealous?" he asked, referring to her mentioning that she had talked to his friends just now.

"I don't know, would you be?" she asked. "Because if you were jealous, that would mean that you cared."

"We slept together," he reminded her.

"That doesn't automatically mean anything," Raegan told him.

Alan did his best to keep a straight face. "Are you impugning my honor?" he asked her. And then he told her a little bit more seriously, "For your information, I don't sleep around."

He held the door open for her.

This time Raegan did smile at what he had just said. "Isn't that supposed to be my line?"

"For your information, that is not a line. I don't take a woman to bed unless it means something to me."

"'Something,'" she repeated. "And by that you mean like having a good time," Raegan presumed.

Alan's eyes met hers. He couldn't shake the feeling that he was looking into her soul.

"Among other things, yes," he allowed.

"Like what?" Raegan pressed. "What other things?"

"You can't figure it out?" Alan asked her. He wasn't trying to sound clever. He had assumed that she would just intuit the answer.

Was he trying to play games with her? "If I

could figure it out, I wouldn't be asking now, would I?" she said, laying the question at his feet.

Alan shook his head. "You have always been a mystery to me, Raegan Robertson. After all this time, I still don't know what goes through your head or what you're actually capable of."

"If I'm so trying—" she began, feeling as if she was on the verge of losing her temper.

Alan held his hand up to stop her before she could get carried away. "I didn't say that. I said you were still a mystery to me—and that's part of what makes you so very interesting."

That stopped her in her tracks. "Just part?" she asked.

"Just part," Alan confirmed. "The other part is that you seem to light up my life with absolutely no effort whatsoever."

And then he stopped walking and sighed.

"What's wrong?" she asked. The expression on his face didn't match what he had just said.

"I wasn't planning on doing this just yet," he confessed.

"Doing what?" Raegan asked, lost…and very afraid to think what was whispering along the perimeter of her mind. This was just wishful thinking on her part, she silently insisted. It had no real place in reality, or in her life. She knew that.

And yet—

And yet she really hoped that it did.

Alan took her hand in his, closing his fingers around it. "This isn't the kind of place I would pick for a proposal."

Her mouth was dry as she asked, "What proposal?" She was convinced that Alan couldn't possibly be saying what it sounded like he was saying.

Could he?

Well, he had gone this far, Alan thought, he couldn't just back out now. That wasn't like him.

"My proposal to you," he answered. "Keep up here, Raegan. I'm trying to ask you to marry me. You don't have to answer right away. You don't even have to give me an answer at all," he added. "Just tell me that you'll think about it."

Raegan's eyes met his. "No."

Alan looked at her, stunned. Well, he had asked for it, hadn't he, he silently thought.

"No," he repeated. "Your answer is 'no.' Just like that?"

"My answer is 'no,'" she told him. "Because I don't have to think about it."

It felt as if he had just been kicked in the gut. It hurt to breathe. "Then I guess there is nothing left to say."

"Yes, there is," she told him. "There's my answer." Taking a breath, she said, "My answer is yes."

Alan blinked. This wasn't making any sense. "Raegan, you've managed to go around in circles and completely confuse me."

She nodded, not taking him to task for his commentary.

"Well, you've going to have to work on that, Alan," Raegan told him. "I don't come with an instruction booklet."

He laughed. "You don't have to tell me that. But just so that we're on the same page, Raegan, your answer to my proposal is 'yes'? This isn't just some kind of a joke on your part, right?"

She put him out of his misery quickly. "Let me assure you that I am capable of much better jokes than that, so, no, this isn't a joke. I will marry you—as long as this isn't a joke on your part," Raegan responded, qualifying her answer.

"The first thing we're going to have to work on is building trust," Alan informed her, grinning. "Agreed?"

Her smile came straight from her soul. "Agreed," she replied.

"All right," he told her, pulling her into his arms

as he drew her close. "Now that that's settled…" he said, his lips coming close to hers.

"Are you going to kiss me right here?" Raegan asked in surprise. He was usually a lot more private than that.

"Right here, right now," Alan told her. "The only thing I don't know is if I'm ever going to stop," he admitted. "Right now, it doesn't look all that likely."

A mischievous smile entered her eyes. "Go for it," Raegan told him.

And he did, intending to continue this intense kiss for a long, long time.

"Well?" Miss Joan asked Holly, the server she had sent to the window to observe what was happening between Raegan and Alan.

Miss Joan had just bid goodbye to the other three engineers she had met through Alan, sending Logan, Chris and Greg off on their journey with a last offering of lunch to tide them over.

Given the circumstances, she was worried about how Alan would react to his friends leaving. And if Raegan would be tempted to try to comfort him.

"He's kissing her—or she's kissing him.

They're kissing each other," Holly concluded. It seemed like the best answer.

Miss Joan smiled now. It was a small smile, but it was there.

"It's about time," the woman commented to herself. "Well, come away from the window," she told Holly. "We don't want them to know they were being observed. At least not until the big day comes."

Holly crossed back to Miss Joan. "Big day?" she echoed.

"Their wedding," Miss Joan answered simply.

Holly shook her head in absolute wonder. "Is there anything that you don't know about ahead of time?" the young woman asked.

Miss Joan had already returned to her work. She merely offered up a mysterious smile. "I'll let you know whenever that happens," she promised with a self-satisfied chuckle. "But it hasn't been known to happen yet."

With that, she prepared to greet Raegan and Alan as the couple was about to walk into her diner.

But just before they came in, the rumble of thunder was heard and then, suddenly, as the sky darkened, rain began to fall in big, fat drops.

"Um, Miss Joan," Holly said uncertainly, "I think it's—it's raining," the server announced.

Miss Joan smiled. "I guess it was a lucky thing that Alan decided to come back to Forever," she said, then chuckled. "He brought the rain."

* * * * *

*Don't miss previous romances
by Marie Ferrarella,
from Harlequin Special Edition:*

Secrets of Forever
Coming to a Crossroads
Her Right-Hand Cowboy
Bridesmaid for Hire
The Lawman's Romance Lesson
Adding Up to Family
The Late Bloomer's Road to Love
The Best Man in Texas

"You still don't belong here." Mariella crossed her arms
over her chest, and Alex commanded himself not to notice
her body, perfect as it was.

"That makes two of us, and yet here we are."

"I was here first," she muttered. He'd heard the argument
before, but it didn't sway him.

"You're not running me off, Mariella. I needed a fresh
start, and this is the place I've picked for my home."

"My plan was to leave the past behind me. You are a
physical reminder of so many mistakes I've made."

"I can't say that upsets me too much," he lied. It didn't
make sense, but he hated that he made her so uncomfortable.
Hated even more that sometimes he'd purposely drive by

her shop to get a glimpse of her through the picture window. Talk about a glutton for punishment.

She let out a low growl. "You are an infuriating man. Stubborn and callous. I don't even know if you have a heart."

"Funny." He kept his voice steady even as memories flooded him, making his head pound. "That's the rationale Amber gave me for why she cheated with your fiancé. My lack of emotions pushed her into his arms. What was his excuse?"

She looked out at the street for nearly a minute, and Alex wondered if she was even going to answer. He followed her gaze to the park across the street, situated in the center of the town. There were kids at the playground and several families walking dogs on the path that circled the perimeter. Magnolia was the perfect place to raise a family.

If a person had the heart to be that kind of a man—the type who married the woman he loved and set out to be a good husband and father. Alex wasn't cut out for a family, but he liked it in the small coastal town just the same.

"I was too committed to my job," she said suddenly and so quietly he almost missed it.

"Ironic since it was your job that introduced him to Amber."

"Yeah." She made a face. "This is what I'm talking about, Alex. A past I don't want to revisit."

"Then stay away from me, Mariella," he advised. "Because I'm not going anywhere."

"Then maybe I will," she said and walked away.

Don't miss
Wedding Season *by Michelle Major,*
available May 2022 wherever
HQN books and ebooks are sold.

HQNBooks.com

New York Times bestselling author

RaeAnne Thayne

brings you a poignant and uplifting novel about forgiveness, family and all the complications—and joy—that come with it.

"RaeAnne Thayne gets better with every book."
—Robyn Carr, #1 *New York Times* bestselling author

Order your copy today!

Love Harlequin romance?

DISCOVER.

Be the first to find out about promotions, news and exclusive content!

 Facebook.com/HarlequinBooks

Twitter.com/HarlequinBooks

Instagram.com/HarlequinBooks

Pinterest.com/HarlequinBooks

YouTube.com/HarlequinBooks

ReaderService.com

EXPLORE.

Sign up for the Harlequin e-newsletter and download a free book from any series at **TryHarlequin.com**

CONNECT.

Join our Harlequin community to share your thoughts and connect with other romance readers!
Facebook.com/groups/HarlequinConnection

HARLEQUIN

Heartfelt or thrilling, passionate or uplifting—Harlequin is more than just happily-ever-after.

With twelve different series to choose from and new books available every month, you are sure to find stories that will move you, uplift you, inspire and delight you.

HNEWS2021